MID-ATLANTIC

Tora Barry

I0445540

Published in 2015 by Castleforge Books Ltd.

ISBN: 978-0-9932939-2-4

Chapter One: Me, My Mother and Ava Gardner

According to my mother, air travel used to be glamorous. "People dressed up to go on planes," she said.

Back then, she showed me a few black-and-white photographs of herself looking like Ava Gardner in tight-waisted dresses and vertiginous heels carrying a little square box with a handle, which was referred to as a vanity case and was taken everywhere as well as a handbag, and in some of the pictures she was wearing a little boxy hat, with a veil. "Oh yes," she said airily when I asked her about it, one rain-and-wine-filled Sunday afternoon "We all looked like that in those days. You made the effort."

At the time, we were sitting in the drawing room of the old house, the one I grew up in, the one before before the horrid bungalow, and before the residential facility, which she referred to as the 'home for retired gentlefolk' although there was nothing gentle about her, or indeed the other folk with whom she shared a sitting room and a small over-tended garden. She was still making the effort then, in a silk shirt with a bow at the neck, and the inevitable pearls.

She looked at my uncomfortable teenaged body, in its cord trousers and baggy sweaters and flat boots, and my unwashed hair tied up in a bundle with an elastic band, and sighed. "God knows what happened to you Joanne," she said, "I just don't know where you get it from."

What would she think if she could see me now? Doing this. She's been dead for six years and I can still hear her, having a go. "What?" she would say, "What? I'm just saying."

I can't imagine what would happen to a hat, boxy or otherwise if it had to go through what I have just had to go through. I know what would have happened to a vanity case because my handbag has just been screened, scanned, rummaged about in, emptied, zipped, unzipped, and photographed. My handbag, if it was a person, would now be very sure it didn't have any sort of disease, or abnormality, in fact it could be confident that it is in radiant health, but it might want to go home and have a bath and put on a dressing gown and lie on a sofa for a while. In passing, I find it strange that an arm or a leg, broken in a road accident, or a sports match, and taken to Casualty, can suffer several hours of waiting painfully in a corridor before it warrants an X-Ray, but a piece of hand luggage can qualify for half a dozen complete scans in the course of a single transit through from Departures to Airside.

But my mother's vanity case wouldn't fit under the seat I'm now sitting in. I know that because nothing at all fits under this seat. I tried stuffing my own squashy, capacious and supposedly flexible bag under there, but it protruded and represented a hazard to other passengers needing to exit the aircraft in an emergency apparently. As this is a window seat, and I am sitting in it, I can't imagine how anybody else would be at risk of becoming entangled in my handbag unless they decided to haul me across their lap in order to sit in this seat, so as to better watch the drama of our crash landing in the sea before attempting an emergency exit, but there you are.

This seat is numbered 60A Window. It is fairly near the front, that is the front of the back, the front of the Economy section, and is distinctly behind (and as this is a Boeing 747, below) Club Class and very distinctly behind the First Class. I am about half a mile away from the pilot, but satisfyingly close to the loo. The Galley is behind the loo and so the convenience of that will depend on whether the crew decides to start from here and work back or vice versa. But the key question is obviously, how close am I to disaster?

Somebody told me once that the safest place to sit on a plane is on the black box because it always survives. But the problem with this is that a) nobody seems to be able to tell me where the 'black box' is situated and b) it conjures up a disturbing image of me, floating alone in the sea for weeks, clutching a black box waiting to be eaten by sharks. Still, at least my loved ones and the flight investigators would have a record of my death, complete with crunching sounds, one imagines, which would be something.

Getting through an airport and onto a plane reinforces my view of myself as ultimately worthless, and not-elegant. I didn't need the airport to make me feel like this, I still have the memory of my mother.

Tucked tidily into my seat, I find there is around me, an air of tension. There is excitement, anticipation, even joy in places. A five year old boy is already driving his own model 747 through other people's personal space, running up and down aisles, tangling his Boden anorak cord in the seat mechanisms and trapping people against other people. But I can also feel that the atmosphere of general thrillingness is cut through with more sinister overtones, apprehension, even fear, and claustrophobia, irritation and frustration, and excesses of many human scents, intentional and unintentional, mingled with hydrocarbons.

For a glorious few minutes I thought that the seat next to me was going to remain empty. Lines of people battled their way onto the plane, brandishing briefcases, and blankets and inflatable pillows and those wheeled cases which are apparently allowed on the aircraft even though I would struggle to fill one even if I packed everything I ever owned, and which trail behind their owners like small cars, weaving their way unheeded into the paths and ankles of unwary followers, who, no matter how hard they try to keep an appropriate distance from the person in front, consistently fail to allow for the half a metre or so of plastic handle length necessary. Coats and scarves and pillows and cases are stowed wildly into overhead lockers before their owners remember that the thing they most want most urgently having taken their seat, is the thing furthest inside the overhead locker.

Right above my head, my own poor bag is now stuffed right at the back of its locker, behind everybody else's plastic carrier bags of gin. I have managed to liberate my book, my reading glasses and a small bottle of water but if I need anything else it will have to wait until absolutely everybody else has collected their stuff and got off the plane. By which time, my linen-mix jacket will be crushed beyond recognition and I will have no time to brush my hair or apply a light dusting of makeup and will be the only person in the line to enter America who actually looks like she has just spent eight or so hours in a washer-dryer on full spin.

And still the seat beside me remained unoccupied.

What a break that would be. A first for me I thought. Getting lucky is not something I am used to.

"You make your own luck in this life Joanne," says my mother, in my head.

I concentrate on trying to make the seat next to me remain empty. Or, better still, I decide, the stewardess will come over and whisper quietly to me that I'm not to make a big deal of it, but if I would like to gather my things and follow her, I can be Upgraded. Upgraded to the soft, music-filled lounge of Club Class passengers, where magazines are new and shiny, and bright green apples sit in bowls on console tables, where champagne is served in real glasses and nobody needs to sit down until they are absolutely ready to do so.

Club Class where there is room to cross one's legs, or sit at an angle, or read a book at the same time as eating a meal, where there are two visual distances instead of only one small one, and one's bifocals are required, because not everything is a maximum of nine inches in front of one's eyes. Club Class where....well never mind. Minutes tick by and my hopes continue to rise.

He arrives, just as the stewardesses are moving down the aisles securing the overhead lockers, telling people off for their protruding handbags and not-absolutely-vertical seat backs.

He is tall, but not offensively so, and well built but not in an overspilling-into-my-seat way. He is wearing a suit, which is good because he looks nice, and bad because it means that if, at the last minute anyone should be upgraded it will be him and not me. Close up, the suit is worn, a bit shiny at the elbows and the cuffs show signs of fraying but although I am close enough to notice it, the Upgrading stewardess will probably not be.

He looks at me. I am not looking at him, but I know he is looking at me because it's his turn to stare, and he has just arrived and it's what I would do if I was him. I can feel his eyes on the top of my head. What is he thinking? I know what he is thinking.

"She is small, which is a good thing, and clean, which is a very good thing. Her clothes are soft, and pastel- coloured, so she is not a businesswoman. She is the wrong generation for a portable electronic device which will vibrate in my ears, and she has a very fat and serious looking book in her lap so she will read and not wish to talk. She looks very tired, so she will probably sleep. If either of us is to be upgraded it will be me."

All in all, I pass the test and when I look up, he smiles.

And there it is. At first I feel pleased. And then I am angry. Why should I feel glad because he thinks I am acceptable? All at once I decide that I no longer wish to be acceptable. All at once, I realise that I have been striving for acceptability all my life. That's what got me into this situation in the first place. That's why I am here, because I have had enough of worrying about whether or not I am acceptable. So I decide that I shall, in fact, be unacceptable. The whole way over the Atlantic. Yes, that is what I shall do, that is what I shall be.

I start by smiling back in what I think is an 'are you single, or looking for an adventure?' kind of way. I might even be doing a little hum. "Hello" I say, in a starting-a-conversation sort of way.

He makes a sort of grunting sound and within a split second has opened a newspaper blocking me out of his line of vision completely. I decide his name is Malcolm, just to spite him, and also to put me off him, just in case.

The doors are closed, the crew is belted into little jump seats, knees together, hands resting in laps, reassuring smiles fixed firmly in place. I feel as though I have been sealed up in a tin, where the air has been sucked out and is being replaced with something altogether more sinister which begins immediately to infiltrate my body, weaving its way into my hair and my ears and working its way into my lungs. I will believe. I will believe in the power of this 400 or so tons of 21st century velociraptor to carry 400 people across an ocean and away, away to a foreign land. I will believe a plane can fly.

Beside me, Malcolm turns the pages of his newspaper, and buries himself in an article about Dave Gilmour of Pink Floyd and how he has invested his massive millions. Malcolm is probably looking for tips about investments rather than about rock music. He pretends to be oblivious. I look at him incredulously. How can anyone not be excited about this? My heart is beating fast, and my hands are gripping the armrests as the plane taxis along the runway, gathering speed, the flat green fields and neat hedges rush past faster and faster, and I can feel the heave and surge as the great lump of a thing lifts, completely improbably, into the air. There is a noticeable outflow of four hundred people's breath, and we are off. And I, I am off too. Off for good.

Half an hour passes, and to be honest nothing much happens. Flying is a curious combination of exciting and boring. The engines hum, a dull rumbling, as the air heats up gradually, being cycled and recycled, filtering through four hundred strangers' bodies, each one taking what little they can from it, until there is no goodness left in it at all. All this conspires to turn even the most intelligent and motivated person (which, incidentally, I am not) into some kind of lemming, following the crowd, mindlessly doing what everyone else does, and scarcely noticing. Most of us, with the exception of Malcolm, spend a pleasant enough half hour working out how the in-flight entertainment systems works while gleefully accepting tiny packets of salted crackers and miniatures of gin from the cabin crew. Malcolm rattles the pages of his newspaper and says no to the crackers, although he does accept two miniatures of whisky.

The TV activated and three episodes of an American sitcom called *My Pal's Penfriend*, later, I can almost stir myself to care about what happens to the main character, who is called Henderson, and his friend Jack's Cuban correspondent, Rita. Yet again I had pledged to use these eight or so hours of inanimate time, of enforced sitting, to read *The Tenant of Wildfell Hall*. I've always meant to read it, yet somehow it remains, stubbornly unread. Copies sit fatly in dusty corners of my life, waiting to make me feel guilty if I open a copy of anything more modern and, frankly, more inviting. And there it was, my latest copy (the Vintage Classics Edition, for those who wish to look for a good copy of their own) stuffed into the seat pocket in front of me, a third of a yard in front of my own nose and as unopened as a rosebud, as raw as a plucked chicken, its several hundred pages of tiny black text as untouched as a Victorian china doll on a high shelf, or in fact, as untouched as I have been for a very long time. Pages which have never even seen daylight. Also rather like me. Up until now.

I am impatient for something to happen. Malcolm is not co-operating. I do what I always do and choose an imaginary world instead of the real one.

In my dreams, a man is sitting three rows behind me. He is wearing an Armani suit, and he is a film director.

"Don't be ridiculous," my mother says. "A film director in an Armani suit would be sitting in First Class."

Nevertheless, there he is. And for some reason, he has decided to sit here, in Economy. In fact, he says he likes being amongst real people actually, enjoys mixing with all levels of society. He feels it connects him with his audiences, inspires his work whilst keeping his roots firmly on the ground. His struggle, for he is a tall man wedged uncomfortably tightly into an aisle seat beside a very large Jamaican lady in full ceremonial dress, who is eating a pie, is essential to his work.

And, he is thinking about his current project, which is a fabulous new adaptation of *The Tenant of Wildfell Hall*, an eighteenth century novel by an English writer Acton Bell, who was in fact a woman, and who was also in fact a Bronte, and if there's one thing Americans love more than Jane Austen, it's a Bronte. And it's going to be filmed in upstate New York, where there are orange woods and blue lakes, and wide skies, and it's all set up. He has Rufus Sewell and he has Tom Hollander and he almost has Colin Firth. With all this manly box-office candy, his concept, pitched at least four years ago now, to a panel of producers and money men round a table in a surprisingly nasty building in Hollywood, permits an unknown female lead. The money men love that idea, as do the box office idols who won't have to share their billing. Critics are already saying it is brave, media types say it's madness, and he, Will Dunstan (Oh look, suddenly he has a name) has faith in his own absolute brilliance. But that was four years ago, and now, in this plane, on his way to the early set build and extras castings and wardrobe fittings, he is sweating a bit because he still hasn't been able to find his Helen Graham.

And little does he know, that just a few rows in front of him, a pale, wide eyed Englishwoman with an inner core of steel, and the sort of (quite bland) face which works so well on camera, is sitting, deep in contemplation of that very literary character. How alike they are, this English woman and Helen, how in tune their feelings, their intuitions, their motivations are, and how time has stood still, up here, 35,000 feet above the ground. Right now, down there, it is possible to imagine it is the eighteenth century all over again. What an extraordinary co-incidence it is, that in an hour or so, he will get up, in order to stretch his legs and thus avoid deep vein thrombosis, stride elegantly up and down the aisle in his English hand-made shoes, and as Ms Bronte would have it, chance upon me, Joanne West, woman of an uncertain age, unknown, mother of one, his Helen.

So I turn reluctantly away from the small-screen Henderson and Jack and Rita, and heave *The Tenant* out of its pocket again.

Across the aisle, Marvin Colton, fifty five, almost 240 pounds, in old Levis and a stolen leather jacket, sweats his way through the miles with the help of repeated shots of Jack Daniels from the trolley. He looks at the fake Rolex on his wrist every half hour and puffs with impatience, as if doing so will make the journey faster. On the screen in front of him, Jack Nicholson is breaking down doors with an axe and women in nightdresses are screaming with blood running down their faces. It is the kind of film Marvin likes, but he can't concentrate. In just a few more hours, he will face the last hurdle. He will get off this plane, stride nonchalantly into the terminal, across the concourses and wait patiently in line to pass through immigration. He will try not to draw attention to himself, a feat of invisibility which is near impossible, given his size and the fact that his shirt is soaked through with his fear. Salt and sugar stick to his front as he packs nuts, crisps and chocolate biscuits into his mouth, as if to keep every muscle, every orifice, every cell busy at once.

He will hand over his passport in a carefree manner, make brief eye contact with the immigration officer, to show he has nothing to worry about, and declare himself an international businessman with a few days to spare for the sights of New York. He may even risk a question such as the best way to get to the Empire State Building, or the overall acreage of Central Park, to demonstrate his complete fascination with the tourist trail.

Then, the immigration officer will grunt, sigh, burp, and stamp the passport, which is so new it could have been forged last week, and wave him through, already steeling herself for the next weary, grey-skinned hopeful in line.

And Marvin Colton will be in. Within half a day he will be across town and across the Hudson River and among new friends, where he will lie low for quite a while.

But that is Marvin Colton's dream, not mine. What will actually happen is quite different I'm afraid. Because Marvin is a murderer. Behind him, east of the east end of London and some way into Essex, is a bungled burglary, at the home of a famous footballer who came home at exactly the wrong time, and got a sawn-off shotgun round in his head for his trouble. And, I'm sorry Marvin, but as if that wasn't bad enough, the footballer, a promising young striker by the name of Precious Adeweybe, was at that very point, being signed by the Russian oligarch who has just bought Hampton Rovers. So if Precious Adeweybe was upset at being murdered, Argon Kristeyvitch was rather more so at being deprived of the inevitable profit he would have made on selling the star player on at the end of the season. And Argon is not a man to let a little thing like that go.

So as Marvin cracks open the little lids of the Jack Daniels bottles with his shaking, sausage-shaped fingers, he has only the faintest idea that at the bottom of the steps which will be wheeled up to the aircraft on arrival at JFK, will be half a dozen of NYPD's finest.

And what they don't know, as they take the calls to get to the airport, divide up their respective roles, check their weapons, and stuff the last of their doughnuts and egg rolls into their mouths, is that as Marvin Colton stands at the top of those aircraft steps, and looks down and sees them, he will die of a heart attack on the spot. Which I suppose, will be some kind of justice. Although it would not have happened to Jack Nicholson.

I congratulate myself on being able, despite my concentration being repeatedly interrupted by dreams of my fellow passengers, to get some way into *The Tenant of Wildfell Hall*. At least you can escape the stresses and strains of real, modern life with great literature. I've got as far as the bit where Gilbert, ignoring the scandalous gossip about his new lodger, takes it upon himself to beat up a man he believes is after her. In my dream, I am completely ready for my close-ups, imagining myself standing beside a stream out in the wild countryside (all copied faithfully in a back lot in a studio in Boston) praying that the size of my bottom in its crinoline costume doesn't eclipse the scenery completely, and am waiting to hear Will Dunstan's sigh of approval, when in reality, I discover that far from the wild, brilliant magnetic character we had imagined Helen to be, we find that she is yet another women taken in and ruined by a seductive philanderer. God, men really are all the same aren't they?

At the back of the plane, Doctor Michael Stevenson is working on a ground-breaking paper he is about to deliver at a conference in New Jersey. The paper is on the latest developments in his work on identifying and isolating the gene which causes Parkinson's disease. At almost forty, he is considered to be the world's second-most respected expert in the field. When Professor Wilkins McKenna of Stanford dies, Michael Stevenson will be the world's leading expert. Wilkins McKenna is seventy eight.

Michael has already refused a drink and a snack in order to concentrate on his work. In a minute however, Michael will have to put his paper aside, because you-know-what will happen again.

It will start with a sort of rustling, a light disturbance of the droning static atmosphere in which we are all trapped, like flies in a jar. The movement is way ahead in the distance, about sixty rows or so, but he can feel that already people are standing up, looking round, scrambling to their feet. Overhead lockers are opened, things pulled hurriedly out. Someone walks quickly forward, pushing past the aisle exercisers, film director Will Dunstan amongst them, who are rolling their ankles round and round and pressing their clasped hands upwards. Then Dr Stevenson sees a flash of red nylon, and then another, and he knows that several crew members have been summoned. He puts the cap on his fountain pen and carefully clips his papers together. It may be some time before he can get back to them. He fishes behind him to the hook where he has hung his lightweight waterproof jacket, tucks his pen into the inside pocket and curses because he has forgotten that at 35,000 feet, even the most expensive fountain pens leak. Then he takes off his reading glasses and replaces them with his walking-about glasses. He drains the bottle of water that he has brought with him, and puts the empty bottle in the seat pocket. Then he waits.

"Good afternoon ladies and gentlemen, this is your Captain, Steve Carlton," says a chocolate-filled voice, all calming reassurance and caramel overtones. Is that our Captain's real name? It is certainly a name to inspire confidence, unlike, say Brian Biggs, or Gordon De'Ath, both of which belonged to boys I was at school with. It is certainly a relief that neither of them is piloting this plane.

"I'm sorry to disturb you at this point," continues my Captain Carlton, "but I wonder if we could call upon anyone with any medical experience to make him or herself known to the crew by pressing the call button located in the panel above your head."

Michael Stevenson presses the button and Shane, in red trousers, a navy and white striped slim-fit shirt and a clip-on tie comes skipping gratefully down the aisle towards him. Returning back up the aisle behind Shane, Michael feels sixty rows of eyes, eight pairs to the right three pairs to the left in every row, row on row, running the gauntlet of blinking worried, interested faces, until he gets to the point just a dozen or so rows ahead of me, where impoverished Park Avenue matron May Wilson, who has already had to endure the indignity of discovering that having spent her entire fortune at the gaming tables, she is now forced to travel economy class, now finds herself falling on even harder times by discovering that she has stopped breathing. Jamie Jones, a very beautiful child-prodigy saxophone player allocated the seat next to her, has stood up and is waving his arms.

As the doctor passes my row, he will look from left to right, and his bedside-brown eyes will catch mine. "I wonder..." he will say, "you look as if...." and he will break off, and I will rise from my seat, climb nimbly over Malcolm and roll up my sleeves.

"Of course," I shall say in my most calm and confident manner, "I should be glad to help you. Now, what should I do?"

Together we will save May's life. We will lift her from her seat and carry her through the magic curtain, flanked by grateful crew, to Club Class (oh, those apples, those sparkling glasses, the space) and we will displace a sleeping oil magnate in order to lie May flat so we can work on her airway, completing an emergency tracheotomy with the plastic outer bit of a biro which I happen to have with me, and Michael Stevenson will look at me in awe and ask me however I learned to do it. And I will smile enigmatically and I will not talk about my hours watching *CSI* or *Midsomer Murders*.

And the crew will smile and relax and open a bottle of champagne for Michael and me, and he will give me his business card and tell me that if I have any interest in his top level conference and if I would like to get involved with his vital research, he would be glad to find a place for me on his team. So we'll sit in Club Class for the rest of the journey and if Malcolm misses me back in Row 60, it will be entirely his own fault for patronizing me on takeoff.

I look at my watch. We've only been flying for an hour and a half. Seven hours to go. I return to *Wildfell Hall*, but I can't concentrate. On the TV screen in front of me Henderson is trying to persuade Rita to cross the Mexican border at the dead of night to meet Jack in a taco restaurant. The hilarity comes from the fact that she claims there is a better taco restaurant on her side.

It's the air. Really, it's the air.

Chapter Two: A Departure and An Arrival

It's rather a long time since I've been to an airport for myself. By which I mean that in the last year I came to Heathrow several times, but on each occasion I was meeting someone else or seeing someone off.

In February I came with Jenna who was dispatching her daughter on a Gap Year. Jenna is my best friend. In reality she is probably my only friend, in the old fashioned sense of the word. Jenna is what she would call a 'police station friend' someone you would call if you found yourself hauled off to a police station in the middle of the night in unexpectedly complicated circumstances possibly involving drink and/or criminal damage. We were at school together, Jenna and I. Jenna is five foot ten in socked feet with almost waist length chestnut hair (yes, she probably does dye it, but she's very good at it, it looks completely natural) and one of those fine elegant faces which manage to covey intelligence, a readiness to move at the speed of light should the occasion demand, and a sort of wistfulness all at once. She's a fashion something. I should hate her because she's all the things I'm not, but from the moment I saw her take a hockey ball from under the nose of my nemesis, Judith Pilkington in the fourth year, and dribble it all the way up the pitch and into the mouth of the goal, her hair streaming behind her and singing at the top of her voice all the way, I decided to love her for being all the things I'm not. Mainly so that I don't have to be any of them.

Jenna's daughter, Seven, who sadly inherited most of her looks from her father and as a result is mainly short and squarish with myopia but is quite the sweetest natured child, will by now be half way down the coast of Chile, on her quest to travel the length of it with a team of other kids who are discovering hitherto undiscovered native crafts. In the meantime, Jenna has bought a motorbike, a Harley Davidson I think, and is sending me text messages from the road. She says she is channeling Jack Kerouac, although I'm not sure it counts if it's in North East England. Meanwhile Rod, Seven's father, carries on as if nothing has happened, playing a banjo-type thing (I called it a banjo once, and was decidedly 'put right' but I can't actually remember what the eventual name for it was) in pubs and clubs, supposedly writing blues ballads, doing the occasional gardening job and generally being absent when needed and present when not.

Back then, we stood at the Departure gate, Jenna and I, our stomachs churning with too much coffee-chain coffee and our brains racing because we had forced ourselves to eat sugary pastry to help with the coffee, and we watched Seven, weighed down by a huge rucksack with a little pink teddy bear attached to the side, as she waited in line to be scanned and X-rayed and suspected of drug smuggling, marvelling at the bravery and freedom of the young, and the wonder of modern global travel and our own sophistication at being quite calm about her only child disappearing into the huge, gaping, open mouth of the wide world. Then, when we couldn't see her any more, despite straining our eyes and craning our necks and pushing people aside from our lines of vision, we went to a bar which smelt of airline carpet and old beer and fear of flying, and we drank a bottle of Jameson's Irish Whiskey between us and then we cried.

More accurately, I cried. "My baby's gone!" I wailed, and Jenna was sweet enough not to point out that Seven was not in fact my baby, but hers. "I may never see her again!" I sobbed.

Around us, weary cleaning operatives swept and wiped and loaded debris from the tables into bin bags.

"She's a free spirit," said Jenna soothingly, "She doesn't need to be actually, physically here to be with us. Just as we don't need to be on that plane, to be with her."

I looked at Jenna through my puffy red eyes, and tried to find some evidence that she was being brave.

"They're only lent to us," she continued. And, do you know, she really believed it.

I've never been able to concur with that sentiment, although I'd heard it many times. From the moment Hugo was born, I knew he was mine. Not somebody else's, lent for a fixed term, rented by the year, the payments increasing as his feet and his appetite got bigger, and then ultimately returnable at some point in the future, delivered back into the air from whence he came. Not even Greg's, although I acknowledged he had some sort of 'visiting rights'. Hugo was mine, and he would be mine for as long as I existed and beyond.

When I got home, much, much later that night, after releasing Jenna into the wild, I found Greg talking about the economy to Hugo, who was watching football. "Hugo's got a second interview," Greg told me in the kitchen, as I headed towards the fridge to boost my flagging Jameson's hangover with Chardonnay. "I've told him how thrilled we are for him."

I looked at Greg and tried to see past the greying hair and that terrible sweater he bought for himself on a whim after decades of expecting me to buy his clothes. I could see that he really was happy about Hugo's job interview, which was with Allied Assurance. Then I looked past my husband into the sitting room, at the top of my son's messy yellow head and beyond it, down the whole distance of him to his great trainered feet and I wondered how it had come to this. My sunny, chunky little friend who wanted to keep leopards in the garden and train fish to read, and who had once invented the perfect speed dinner combining pasta and peas and ice cream, had grown so long, and so far, that now, his father seemed to believe that his best plan was a job at Allied Assurance. I thought about Seven, all those miles up above South America, a child the same age as ours, who had grown up alongside him, had played in the same gardens, and swum in the same pools, had gone to the same school and who had been the substance of more than one of my fantasies of marriage for Hugo, and who now bathed in glorious technicolour half way round the world, and I wondered what I had done wrong. "That's great!" I said, "Very encouraging. I've got some chops for supper."

I wonder what I would have done if I had known that I was just days away from the discovery which would change my life forever. I wonder if I would have bothered with the chops.

In June, I went back to the airport, this time to collect Colin Pitt. Greg had been at great pains to tell me it was pronounced Coh-Linn, in an American-annoying way, and Pitt as in Brad. "Really?" I said.

I arrived in plenty of time, and parked the car about a mile up on the roof of the car park, near the place where the luggage trolleys should be but never are. I'd promised Greg I wouldn't be late to meet the plane, and as Colin was coming in from San Francisco on the appropriately named 'red-eye' I'd had to get up unfeasibly early to do it. By the time I'd got as far as the Arrivals Hall, it was eight thirty in the morning and I already felt as though I'd done a day's work. Why do perfectly sensible shoes, which you have happily worn for days on end around the house and the village and the local supermarket, start to rub agonizingly as soon as you are just far enough away not to be able to go back and change them?

So I got myself a coffee from the same coffee outlet Jenna and I had spent so much time in earlier in the year, and a pastry, although I knew I would regret it as soon as I had eaten it, but at the time I had no idea how much I would wish for those 400 calories to be taken back. And I looked out at the concourse from my slightly raised, carpeted platform and I watched people arriving at Heathrow from all over the world.

Airports are dangerous places. For me, I mean. No sooner do I get inside a Terminal Building, engulfed in the yellow-lit, trolley-weary, overexcited tide of humanity, and I smell the synthetic air filled with particles of nylon luggage and the dust of a thousand foreign countries, than I take on a mood of recklessness no less perilous than that of a woman on the roof of a very high building who thinks she can fly.

I scan the boards, looking up and down and hearing the names of destinations in my head, and wondering how long it would take to get there. Montenegro, Paraguay, Paris, St Petersburg, Atlanta, Antwerp. These days I know I'm no longer a child because I also wonder how much it would cost. What clothes would I need? I could probably buy everything else at Boots in the Departures

Lounge. There's a foreign exchange bureau just over there (although of course Greg says it's quite the most expensive way to change money, and airport bureaux de change should be avoided at All Costs). I could get a ticket using this credit card which I have here in my hand. I could go. I could just stand up, put my jacket on, walk over to that ticket desk, speak for a matter of moments to that man in his green uniform, and I could go.

At nine o clock on the unseasonably hot June morning however, I was in Arrivals, so I was distanced a bit from the greatest source of danger. Instead I contented myself with watching all the people flooding into England.

Greg says you can tell what language a person is speaking by watching the shape of his mouth when he speaks, even if you can't hear the words. Using this method I identified a small delegation of French businessmen, but as they passed me, I heard them talking about Wolverhampton Wanderers in English with Midlands' accents which was curious.

I had checked the board for the incoming San Francisco, and at the appropriate time I positioned myself in the line-up of cab drivers and grandparents with 'Welcome Home' signs, all ready to await Colin Pitt. Greg had texted several times to make sure I was in the right place and wearing the right clothes and as he put it, giving the right impression. So I was wearing a jersey wrap dress which, like all wrap dresses promises much in the way of sensationalising curves but in reality, as soon as you've had it on for more than a minute, clings to you like an oil slick and shows what you look like underneath, complete with underwear labels. So I looked vaguely saggy above the waist and as solid as concrete below it, with just a hint of bulge halfway down my thighs where my Amazing

Sculptural Pants ended and my Less Amazing Real Flesh was allowed to roam free. My hair was frizzing unattractively with the heat, and I waited patiently, holding my small and painstakingly coloured-in sign with Greg's company logo on it. I scanned the waves of incoming passengers, the weary businessmen, the prodigal children with their backpacks, the flamboyant guys fresh from Fashion Week, or Hairdresser Week or whatever, about sixty Japanese men in transit, a small film crew with a tremendous amount of luggage, a pop star I vaguely recognized, and then, all of a sudden, there he was. Colin Pitt. But more of him later.

Chapter Three: How Do You Know You're Ready?

Several of my friends (I use the term loosely, as we already know, Jenna is the only proper friend I have, but of course I do still have some social contacts), have decided that their mid-forties are the beginning of the end. They are planning the weddings of their children, looking forward avidly to babysitting their grandchildren, and downsizing their houses, favouring fewer stairs, smaller gardens, and nearby bus routes. I don't think I really started to panic until I read a series of Facebook posts from someone who had been at my primary school with me and with whom I had long lost touch. In her lively stream of consciousness, she wrote delightedly about herself as 'Nanny' and her husband, a telecomms engineer barely halfway through his career, as 'Gramps', and posted pictures of themselves holding toddlers on beaches. Is that it? I thought, and in the words of the great Peggy Lee, *Is That All There Is*?

I told Jenna, who threw back her head of new pink highlights and roared with laughter when I showed it to her. "That woman," she said, pointing at the timeline, or what she referred to as the 'Back in Time Line', "Was seventy the day she was born. She's done nothing with her life, and now she's just bustling through, waiting for it to end, and fuelling the wait with good deeds and cups of tea."

"I've done nothing with mine either," I pointed out.

Jenna took rather longer to respond to this than I had hoped.

"I haven't seen the world, saved any lives, had a big career, won any awards, I haven't done anything which made a difference!" I wailed.

"So far" said Jenna. "Not everyone is supposed to be a world-changer. But just because you aren't Bill Gates or Richard Branson or Hilary Mantel, or Paula Rego or Sir Robert Winston, or..."

"Stop!" I cried, "Stop listing all the brilliant people I am not. You're making it worse. I'm nobody. And I'm not sure I want to get ready for the end of my life, knowing that I'll always be nobody."

"You've done lots of really good things" Jenna began again.

"Yeah?"

"You've had some interesting jobs. And you are good at baking. And you've been a great wife to Greg."

"For what it's worth," I muttered, blackly. "After all where did that get me?"

"Well, it got you Hugo. You made him. You put another new human being on the Earth. Maybe he'll be the life changer, and it will be down to you."

"Life changer by proxy?" I said doubtfully, thinking of Hugo and imagining him behind a desk at Allied Assurance, filling out claims forms and planning what to eat at the firm's Christmas Dinner, months in the future.

"There's still time." Jenna said. "Maybe the thing you were born to do is just around the corner."

"If I believed that, I would have a crick in my neck from just looking round corners," I said. "And don't say Mary Wesley."

"Well why not? She didn't publish her first novel until she was seventy, and then she went on to write loads more and everyone loved them. And Laura Ingalls Wilder, the *Little House on the Prairie* woman? Her first book was published when she was sixty-five."

"I'm not sure I'm going to make it to sixty-five at this rate. I might just lie down and die of worthlessness."

"Colonel Sanders then."

"What?"

"Colonel Sanders. The chicken bloke. He was fifty when he created the secret recipe."

"Great. I've got five years to invent some seriously bad food and twenty to write a bestseller. I'll get onto it."

"You may joke Darling, but there is truth in what you say," Jenna said. "We learn by experimenting. And experimentation takes time. And truthfully, you haven't really started experimenting yet have you?"

I thought about Greg, and Hugo, and the house, and looked inside the wardrobe of gentle classics that was in my head, and metaphorically selected a beige cashmere sweater which went with everything. I wondered what 'Nanny and Gramps' would invent if they started experimenting.

"You should be too busy for Facebook anyway." said Jenna.

Chapter Four : Displacement Activity for the Modern Wife

What do you do all day? When your baby has gone off to secondary school (or, in reality, to the shopping centre to hang out with other truant-playing youngsters disinclined to sit through Double RE) and your husband has gone to work (or, in reality, to Sunderland to have an affair in the afternoons with a blonde PR girl called Vanilla) and your best friend is hanging out with fashionistas in a tent in Milan, and you've already washed the kitchen floor?

There is a space in every woman's life, situated neatly just after you hand over the keys to your car to a huge boy who you remember being twelve years old but has just inexplicably passed his driving test, and just before you sign your final divorce papers, when you realize that you no longer recognize any of the people you live with. You sit there, across the breakfast table, or the newly-carpeted sitting room, and you see grown men and women where there used to be babies, and you see another man who reminds you of someone you used to know but who is much older, and somehow emptier than the one you remember.

That man, the one you knew a long time ago, used to call you several times a day to tell you pointless incidental things, and from this you deduced that he loved you. He used to bring you things, like flowers, and buns, and he picked up special stones for you when you were on the beach together, and he left stuffed toys in hilarious places for you to find, and he spent hours making you compilation tapes of your favourite love songs. That man always had interesting things to say, and you talked to him for hours and hours and hours, and you never even thought about turning the television on. That man cooked for you, rustling up omelettes like Michael Caine in *The Ipcress File*, and roast lunches, and his signature Spaghetti Bolognese, to impress you. That man captured your imagination.

Whereas this man, the one you now have seated at your kitchen table every morning and evening, calls you once a day to ask you if you've remembered to wash his favourite sweater or to go to the tip with the broken rotary clothes line, or to tell you he's going to be late. He sometimes brings you a bottle of wine which he drinks himself, he asks other people to send you flowers on his behalf but only because he's forgotten your birthday, and he wouldn't know what your favourite love song was if you played it at a thousand decibels through a loudhailer attached to the roof of your car. (Unless you had it played over the tannoy at a football stadium, when he might complain that Billy Joel's *She's Always a Woman to Me* was interfering with his enjoyment of the collective rendering of 'Ref, You Are a Sodding Wanker' from the terraces). This man never says anything at all, and you are relieved when he turns the television on because at least then you stand a chance of having somebody from the outside world put some effort into your evening. Assuming there isn't a match on. This man can sometimes be persuaded to bring home a take-away, although he always mistakes bhuna (which you like) for korma (which you don't).

This man thinks less about capturing your imagination and more about the amusing possibilities of capturing farts under a duvet.

I thought about going back to work. Years ago, when I was in my twenties, straight after a disappointing spell at art college, I used to be a thing called a stylist, on a lifestyle magazine. Every Monday morning, I went to a meeting where journalists and editors would decide what stories they were going to cover, and what sort of pictures they wanted, and I would collect together all the things they wanted to take pictures of, and arrange them in a clever and unusual way. Sometimes the things were easy to find, glass, vases, dinner services, cushions, things like that, and sometimes they were more of a challenge. I once spent twenty four hours looking for a piece of pink marble for a piece on Venetian Bathrooms, during which time I spoke to a lot of lovely Italian men. Another time I had to recreate a complete kitchen, all in black, for something to do with vampires. I still have the photographs somewhere.

Greg called it being paid to go shopping.

I considered going back to work, in the same field. "Hello" I said on the phone, "I wonder if any of the people I used to work with are still at this number? I wonder if you have any opportunities for an experienced freelance stylist? I'm very good with colour and light and spatulas." And the people I was speaking to sort of laughed, because stylists are called editors these days, and nobody who works on a magazine is over twenty, and most of them are on what is now apparently called 'internships' which means they work for nothing. And although I don't need the money, and I told them I would be glad just to have something to do, they seemed to think that still didn't make me right for them. And they wished me luck with my search.

So then I wondered what else I could do with my days. Firstly, I shopped, making full use of my apparently unwanted skills. I began by buying things for the house, I re-carpeted, had new curtains made, chose plates and vases, and once, notably, a conservatory. But when I found myself almost enjoying an afternoon on a trading estate in Cowley, seriously comparing hot tubs, I realized I was just filling in time.

Then I rethought my wardrobe. I invested in a new look, and then, when I found that 'Pirate' wasn't a good look for me, I bought into 'rock chick' before going for 'bohemian and artistic', narrowly missing 'mother of the bride' and 'building society manageress', and ending up at 'depressed housewife whose life is completely devoid of activity or meaning, and is now servicing quite a high level of credit card debt'.

"I have the answer," said Jenna, who was on the phone from Cairo. I didn't ask why she was there, or what she was doing.

"The answer to what?" I said.

"To why there isn't any meaning in your life."

"I didn't exactly say there wasn't any meaning in my life!"

"Yes you did. You nearly bought a hot tub."

"It was a very good deal! And I think it would be relaxing."

"You don't need to relax. You need to stop relaxing. You need to do something exciting."

There was a silence.

"Go on then," I said eventually. "Tell me what I need to do."

"You need to have an affair," said Jenna.

"Oh Good," I said, "Where do I start?"

"I'm serious!"

" Well I'm not," I said, "I can't think of anything worse. All that creeping about and lying and whispering, and anyway, nobody would fancy me, and I don't fancy anybody, and besides, what would it do to Greg?"

"You can't think of anything worse, because you haven't found the object of your affair yet. Sex is always dreadful when it's taken out of context. Trust me sweetheart, you just keep an open mind, and open eyes, and do something about your hair, and very soon, a candidate will appear on the horizon, and you will take one look and you will decide that there is nothing worse than not having him. And if you want my opinion, it would do Greg the world of good to realize that even if he doesn't appreciate you, there are plenty of men who would."

"What's wrong with my hair?" I said.

"Nothing. In principle," Jenna said, "It just needs doing."

"It's been done. I do it every day. I wash it and brush it, and sometimes I use a good conditioner on it!"

"It needs doing by somebody else," said Jenna.

"Why are you in Cairo anyway?" I said. But Jenna had rung off.

I thought about Jenna's suggestion, (affair, not hair) really I did. Let nobody say I'm incapable of keeping an open mind. And I started looking hopefully at men when I was out, as a sort of trial run. I looked interested in whatever it was they were looking at, or talking about. I smiled appreciatively when I saw a nice-looking, well-dressed one. I said 'Hello' to a few and made hilarious comments while accidentally-on-purpose brushing against them by car park payment machines. Most of them looked frankly, quite scared.

So then I looked elsewhere for inspiration. What would Princess Grace have done? I asked myself.

What would any of the women who inspire me do? What would Virginia Woolf do? (Perhaps Virginia wasn't ideal, on this occasion, thinking about it). What would Kate Adie do? Fay Weldon? Jenni Murray?

I don't think I consciously thought of Delia Smith, but somehow, I turned to baking. I baked cakes, and casseroles, and buns, and bread, and pies. And everyone within a mile of me got fatter, including the woman next door whom Hugo referred to as 'the chubster' and the vicar, who invariably ate at least half of everything anybody donated to the village fete.

Fairly soon, it became apparent that unless I planned to get involved in online gambling, or any other activity that can be done in the house whilst wearing a stretch towelling dressing gown, my next obsessional activity should involve some sort of diet. So I made charts and set goals, drew progress path documents and accessorised them with pictures of other fat people, sticking them to the fridge with magnets bearing motivational statements. I ate carbs and then no carbs, followed by wheat and no-wheat, and then soup, and then biscuits, and then I did the South Beach diet, and the Palm Beach Diet ("up next, the Beached Whale", suggested Hugo), and the Parisian Women Never Get Fat diet, and the Fat Round the Middle diet, and eventually the You Are What you Eat diet, which threw up (no pun intended) a bit of a conundrum, because over about six months I had eaten everything and nothing, which you might say, was indeed something of a Metaphor for Me.

And finally, I had run out of displacement activity. I drifted through the day, wandering in and out of bookshops, saw a few films and dreamt about being Someone who Did Something Interesting, and in the end I did the only thing which was left to do.

Which was nothing. And just as I got really good at it, Something Happened.

Chapter Five : Things You Have to Leave Behind

The thing about packing is that there comes a point when, because you know you can't take everything, you don't want to take anything. I stood on the landing of my once-loved house, and looked at the doors which led into the rooms and I knew without going in, the precise place of every piece of furniture, every angle, every item of clothing, every repeating pattern of wallpaper or curtain fabric, the sound of the floors and the window catches and doors opening, and the smell of the air which waited patiently, all day and all night, for me to decide, as and when I was ready, to walk in.

So many events had left their mark on the atmosphere of each room. The marks of Hugo's growing on the door frame of his room, and the vague, mysterious smell of unwashed boy inside it. The giggles and sniffles and tears still hung in the air of the main, once our, bedroom. There were echoes of shouting reverberating up and down the stairs, and the chatter and polite conversation of guests in the sitting room. Even in the garden I could see the past, a marquee for my fortieth birthday party, in which speeches were made and wine was drunk and middle-aged spread danced to the music of time.

Whenever there was just me in it, it seemed impossible to imagine that there were sometimes more of us in the house. With me, and the quiet and the air and the books and papers and cushions and cooking things, the house seemed just full enough. But then Greg would come home and put his briefcase on a chair and leave his shoes in the middle of the floor and his newspaper on the kitchen table, and somehow the house would expand a bit and there would just about be room for him, although there were times, especially recently, when it felt unbearably crowded, and then Hugo would drop out of college again, or lose a casual job, or get dumped by a flatmate who found a live-in girlfriend, and come back to live with us, and somehow the house seemed to expand even further to accommodate him and his holdall full of crumpled clothes and bike magazines and books he never read. And I loved having him around, but sometimes the rooms and the floors and the furniture, even the air, just seemed to get very overused.

I made a list of the things I would take with me, if I could: My full length red velvet coat, bought in a street market in Paris in 1985. My leatherbound copy of HE Bates *The Darling Buds of May*. My ingredient-spattered *Complete Works of Elizabeth David*. The pretty, pale straw-coloured sitting room carpet. The view over the Chilterns from the bathroom window. Greg's blue-on-blue Turnbull and Asser shirt. The day we all went to the races, at Newbury, in 1996, when Hugo was five. My recording of Mario Ancona and Enrico Caruso singing the duet from *The Pearl Fishers*. And the beautiful sandals which lace up all across the foot and up the ankle and have a four inch heel that I bought in Spain when I was drunk and which I have never worn because I can fall over on a level carpeted surface wearing flats and have never been able to so much as stand in a heel. The sandals hang from a doorknob in my bedroom to remind me that if I want to be, I can be the kind of woman who wears beautiful shoes.

And that's about it. And, as I sat and looked at my small going-away forever bag, and I knew that none of the things I really wanted could go with me, I almost changed my mind about going at all.

So I went downstairs again and set about treating myself to a cup of extremely nice coffee, Greg is a stickler for good coffee and scours Saturday markets and delicatessens and Fortnum and Mason for obscure and marvellous beans, which I feel guilty about using when he is not here. The freezer is full of them, bags of dark shiny beans, all tagged and labeled by Greg with the name of the roast variety, the date of purchase, and the exact weight. I emptied the bag into the grinder and then I replaced the beans in the freezer with some ordinary ones I'd bought from the supermarket. The kitchen filled with the aroma of lovely coffee, but then coffee's deceptive like that. The smell of coffee is completely different from the taste. On this occasion, the resulting cup, ground, filtered, plunged and poured into a favourite mug tasted nice, but really quite ordinary. I wondered if I had already done the swapping the beans in the freezer thing and was now reaping what I had sown. The eventual disappointment of deception.

Then I turned on the TV in the kitchen where as luck would have it, Angela Rippon was demonstrating a capsule wardrobe. Not a very small cupboard you understand, but a collection of ten or so items of clothing which combine to represent about a hundred outfits, and include something suitable for every eventuality. Well not potholing probably, although there are some lightweight waterproof trousers. And will I be potholing? In this future of mine? Angela is the kind of woman who could go potholing in white trousers and still emerge looking as though she had been browsing the perfume counters in Harvey Nichols. Well informed, well turned out, and untouchable. Newsreader non-stick-chic.

Sitting at my kitchen table, I wondered if this was the last time. Would I ever sit there again, looking round this really quite nice room, would I open the fridge ever again, or the oven, or struggle with the cutlery drawer that has never opened properly, or rummage under the sink for rubber gloves or the dustpan, and would I ever clear dead wasps off the windowsill again, and would I mind if I couldn't see the frowning beaky face of the horrible chicken jug which Greg's mother gave me for Christmas once, many years ago?

It was already late September, but out in the garden the sun was still hanging on. It was pale and hesitant, apologetic in the face of imminent autumnal wind, and nothing like as yellow as I would have liked. As a result, the light here in the kitchen was cool and flat, and I could see the visitors of ten years sitting here like ghosts, mugs, forks, wine in hand, and hear the conversations of thousands of breakfasts, lunches and evenings, rattling round the empty room. Here Jenna and I had wailed about formula baby milk and pureed carrots and nursery schools. Here Greg and I battled with our respective days' work and gave each other support and advice and made holiday plans and drew pictures of the extension we never built and made promises we couldn't keep. And here Hugo dumped his schoolbags and his shoes and bits of his bicycle, and hoovered up huge sandwiches and pints of juice with his mates. Here we all sat on Friday evenings, trying to behave like a civilized proper family, and struggling to make sense of our diverse weeks, Hugo desperate to get away to the computer or the phone, or the TV, Greg and I drinking more   and more until we could eventually allow ourselves to admit we were just tired out.

When I was a child, I wanted, like lots of other little girls, to be a *Blue Peter* presenter. When I was that child, the presenters were Valerie Singleton and then Lesley Judd and Janet Ellis. They were old enough to be my mother, or at least the younger, friendlier mother of one of my friends. At the time, I doubted I would ever be old enough to be a *Blue Peter* presenter. And then, suddenly, one day I turned on the television in the middle of the afternoon (it's alright, I was doing the ironing), and there was *Blue Peter,* and all the presenters were teenagers. In an instant, somewhere between yesterday and the ironing, I had gone from being too young, to being too old.

As I sat there, on through the morning, I saw Jenna again in my head, this time a few years later, worrying about Seven and whether she was ready for boys. First she didn't seem to have a boyfriend, then she did have one but we didn't like him. She wanted her ears pierced, or her hair dyed, or to wear make-up. She wanted to be grown up. So do we! we wailed into our Chianti, when do we get to be grown up, to do grown up things? Because it seemed as though one minute we were kids, too busy with homework, too told off by everyone and everything, and then in an instant, we were too tied down, with men, children, houses. When will we be granted freedom? we cried.

The truth of it is, that nobody can give you freedom. Freedom is something you have to take. And what would we have done, back then, with all that freedom? Looking back I can see that Jenna began collecting it from that point, depositing little amounts of it into a central account, establishing routines of what modern women call 'me-time' whilst appearing to be completely committed to man and child and the PTA committee. Jenna saved up her freedom and when there was enough of it, she bought a huge big chunk of me-time and off she went and nobody was surprised or upset or challenged or disappointed. They were used to her claiming her life for herself. Whereas I filled my freedom bank with extra pointless commitments that nobody noticed, and told myself that I was busy. And when I looked for it, all that time later, it wasn't there. I couldn't even join an evening class, painting, dancing, jazz singing, because it was bound to clash with someone else's schedule. Somebody needed picking up or dropping off, or cooking for, or needed my vote on a tiny, inconsequential issue.

I was jealous of Jenna. I wanted to hate her for leaving me, for making me the plus-one in her life too. I was always the plus-one, the one who was asked to go along with someone else, who stood and watched, or carried bags, or sat on a single seat while someone else impressed on a stage. I was used to being good about being cancelled at the last minute, while more important things came up for other people. "It doesn't mean I don't love you," they said, "I'd much rather be with you," and worst of all, "It's not you."

It was never me. That was the point.

Then, as I sat there, with my indifferent coffee at my kitchen table, my packing more or less done, I could see Lucie, sitting opposite me. That was a surprise, I thought I had managed to rub her out of my memory. Lucie at nineteen. So, that would be a year ago. It was before we redecorated. I know that because the walls I can see in my head are terracotta, which was terribly fashionable at the time we did it, and then retro for a couple of years, and hopelessly shabby after that until the bit I shall call After Lucie, when I drove to B and Q at six thirty in the evening and bought gallons of paint in a shade called Smoked Trout, (which is a sort of mauvy brown), and stayed up all night covering the kitchen walls with a roller and a lot of attitude. The paint is really thick in places. Underneath, there are words, written in huge letters. You can't see them but I can.

Even as I remembered her, when I was all by myself, and she was bathed in the glow of hindsight, Lucie was still beautiful. All shiny with youth, and smiling lovely teeth. She was wearing that pale blue shirt, the one she wore the first time she came to the house. Too many buttons of it were undone, and so I, standing up beside her could see right down to her bra which was black and lacy. Presumably Greg and Hugo could see it too. She was terribly friendly and polite. Later Greg and I would agree that she seemed like a very well-brought up girl and we were quite pleased with Hugo for asking her to supper, although secretly a bit guilty, because we thought he might be punching a bit above his weight. Greg said he just hoped Hugo wouldn't get hurt, which became rather ironic quite soon afterwards. Lucie came round for supper quite a few times after that first visit, and once she even came for Sunday lunch.

I'd made a special effort with the lunch, a nice piece of some animal or other, I forget which, they all seemed rather to merge into one after a thousand Sundays in the kitchen, but I know I did three vegetables, and a decent bread and butter pudding, because I always did that for guests. During the pre-lunch drinks I noticed Greg making an effort to talk to her, and I was pleased they were all getting on so well. Hugo had never brought a girl home before, and to be honest I wondered if he was a bit wary of women. So it was lovely to see them all chattering away over lunch. They refused to let me clear up because I'd cooked, so I went into the garden with the last of the wine, and fell asleep in a deckchair. When I woke up, Hugo was in the chair next to me.

"Dad's taken Lucie home," he said."I think she had a bit too much wine with her lunch."

I laughed. "Poor girl. I expect she was nervous, meeting her boyfriend's parents."

"She's met you before," Hugo pointed out.

"I mean properly. Officially. Over a proper lunch."

Hugo looked at me oddly. "What's to be nervous about? It was only a chicken."

"You don't understand how we women feel," I told him. "These things are important. She will have wanted to give a good impression."

"She's not my girlfriend Mum," Hugo said, and I smiled at him indulgently and said he didn't have to worry, I wasn't about to pry into his sex life. It might have been my imagination, but looking back on it, I wonder if he actually winced.

After that, Lucie came round quite a few times. Sometimes she would drop in when Hugo was out and I was so pleased with myself for having the kind of house that is welcoming to a young woman who is dating my son, and for being the kind of woman who can get along with people from another generation in my own right.

Of course what I didn't realize until later, much, much later, is that she was also dropping in when I was out.

Even Jenna was surprised and she's much more a woman of the world than I am. "Good Heavens," she said. "Seven would never do a thing like that." And then there was a silence as we realised we had no idea whether Seven would seduce a man who was not only old enough to be her boyfriend's father but actually was her boyfriend's father. And in all probability, if asked, Lucie's mother probably had no idea what her daughter was up to either.

Boys are supposed to be close to their mothers aren't they? Girls and their Dads, boys and their Mums? We were close too, Hugo and I, but not for very long. Somewhere between the Lego and the Nintendo I realised there were things I didn't know about Hugo's world. Closed doors. Underpants I hadn't bought. A haircut from someone who wasn't Antonio in the High Street. When did my child become another whole person?

Hugo found out about Lucie and Greg because I told him. I felt terrible about having to do it, but after a while of not telling him, I realised it was getting bigger and bigger until I couldn't see round it, and I couldn't see the television, or the cooker or the way to the bathroom. An elephant of such proportions it threatened to explode at the slightest touch and wipe us all out.

He sat for a bit, staring into his mug of tea. I thought he might be crying but when he finally looked up, his eyes were just sad.

"Try not to be angry with your Dad," I said, because I couldn't bear to think of anger of any kind in my beautiful sunny son. "He's just going through some kind of mid-life crisis I expect. And Lucie, well, she's probably looking for a father at the minute. Lots of girls go through these things when they're young..."

"Mum!" Hugo cut me off in mid-benevolent sentence. "I'm not angry with Dad. Or Lucie. I didn't like her much anyway. She just sort of tagged along with me. Now we know why. I'm not surprised, to be honest with you."

"I'm glad you aren't angry," I said, "Anger can be so negative." I realised I was looking at the knife rack with something approaching professional interest.

"I didn't say I wasn't angry," he said, standing up and putting his mug down on the table with unexpected force, so the tea slopped over the side. I resisted the temptation to leap up for a cloth, but worried inwardly about the effect of the liquid on the wood.

"I'm angry with you," he said. "It's your fault. You're so nice. You're so bloody naive. You just let this stuff happen Mum."

And he left the room.

This morning, sitting there for that final hour with the last of my swindled coffee going cold in its mug, I could still see Lucie next to me at my kitchen table, all bouncy swingy hair and slim hips and sex with my husband. So as she wasn't going anywhere, I had to. I left the mug on the table for her to put away and went back upstairs to design a capsule wardrobe for myself, using some basic ingredients and quite a lot of lateral thinking.

On the way up I was distracted by that row of framed photographs I had hung on the stairs all those years ago. They're all of Hugo, taken a year or so apart, by the same photographer. I used to look at them all the time, but in recent years they sort of faded into the fabric of the house, like wallpaper or door handles, and I had somehow, along the way, stopped actually noticing them.

When Hugo was small people used to say he looked like me. But now I realize that they probably just said that to please me. People speaking to Greg probably told him how much his son looked like him. In reality, Hugo is quite an even mix . He has my chin, which is quite square, and my mouth, which is quite small, and with which I have always been reasonably satisfied. He has his father's hair though, all those fair wavy chunks which never seem to lie straight. And his eyes are blue, which is interesting because mine are grey and Greg's are brown. The year Seven did basic genetics in Biology at school, she was about eight I believe, she told me most earnestly that it is entirely possible for a grey-eyed parent and a brown-eyed parent to produce a blue-eyed child which, I informed her, put my mind at rest. I mean, as I said to her, I knew he was mine of course, and I knew he was Greg's because I hadn't slept with anyone else for years and years, but there was always the possibility of the hospital mix-up, or the alien changeling thing. Seven was very clear about all that. "Phew!" I said, and she looked up at me, all serious and concerned and said "You must have been so worried."

There's Hugo at eight, the same age as that budding geneticist, still sweet, freckles just appearing, with his frown, as though he was forever trying to work something out which was very difficult, and his little blue and white striped Breton sweater the year we went to France on holiday. Then there he is at nearly ten, as awkwardness crept in and he began to care what he looked like. By twelve, he is much longer, and frankly more alien than child, with scowling eyes and unbrushed hair and a black T-shirt that he refused to take off. That's the last one of the photographs, because he rebelled after that and Greg said we had to respect his decisions. So there's no record of the thinnest phase, or the punky one, when the hair was purple, or the first time he wore his little professorish glasses. And no record of the point at which the new one appeared, the one which threatens to be permanent, the vague, gentle, and slightly hopeless one, who changes direction with the wind, and wears sweaters which hang off him, and who just sort of drifts, in and out of rooms. But all the Hugos are in my heart, all the ones he has been and all the ones he is and all the ones he ever will be, so that's alright.

I left the suitcase by the front door while I checked the house for open windows. After all, I had no idea when anyone would be back. I almost tripped over the bag a moment later, which made me think of something Greg had said, a long time ago. "You don't really live in this marriage do you?" he said, "You're just staying over. You're always packed, ready to leave."

He was speaking metaphorically of course. And he was also speaking with something of a forked tongue, because if he was right, and I was always – metaphorically - standing next to my emotional baggage by the front door, then metaphorically – someone else was bringing her own, rather lighter (probably Louis Vuitton) baggage, into my house by the back door. And because I was looking out at the drive, planning some kind of break for the border, I just didn't see it coming.

Is it better to have known and lost than never to have known at all?

In my suitcase, for the benefit of those who have yet to achieve the perfect capsule wardrobe: A big white shirt. Two T-shirts, one black and one white(ish) A fistful of assorted items of underwear (old, non-matching). One pair of jeans. One pair of crease-free black trousers, (not suitable for potholing) One beaded skirt, pinkish red. One dress, stretchy all purpose, black. One very battered much-loved and much-too-young-for-me denim jacket. One more sensible tweedy green jacket. One CD of Mario Ancona and Enrico Caruso singing the duet from *The Pearl Fishers,* and one completely impractical and very heavy long red velvet coat. Angela Rippon would be so proud.

Chapter Six : A Treatise on Queueing

On today's trip to Heathrow, the taxi driver dropped me with unseemly haste outside Departures, anxious to get started on the battle of a thousand lanes, which would allow him to drive round the building and up to Arrivals, where he could pick up a lucrative fare to Kent, or Somerset, and render his day's work profitable. As he roared off, leaving me and my one romantically battered holdall on the pavement in a cloud of diesel fumes, I felt as though my last connection with Life as I knew it had been severed. He was a cab driver and a very uncommunicative one at that, but by the time we had made our way from the-place-which-used-to-be-called-Home, through the lanes and across the M4 to Heathrow I felt as though we were almost family. After all, I had already given away my actual family. So Bernard, as the laminated licence on his dashboard proclaimed his name to be, Bernard with the two gap-toothed freckled, pinkish-haired children who accompanied him along the length of the glove compartment, Bernard with the Christmas Tree air freshener (in September) well, he was all I had. And when he left me, so unceremoniously, I have to say I felt bereft.

Inside the building, I stood, one of an army of a thousand supplicant pilgrims, all side by side, all looking up, our eyes cast toward heaven, our faces lit green by the combined white strip lighting and the yellow of the airport signage. We could all have been chanting, Hail O Great One, O Great Board of

Information, Look Down Upon Us and Smile with your Wondrous Benevolent Greatness and Convey To Us the appropriate Check-In information. At our feet was a mass of luggage, of boxes and cases tied with string and those jaunty rainbow-coloured straps with names woven into them and tiny little combination locks which would cause but a moment's inconvenience to a thief with a penknife, and squashy sports bags stretched beyond limits. We had skis and golf clubs and we had scuba gear and musical instruments, and one of us had a plasma screen television in an enormous box. We looked up and up and up, and a mouse could have run freely around our feet without any of us noticing.

One by one, we received the information we sought, and, reclaiming our personal little bagged worlds, holding tight to all we had, we started to weave our multitudinous paths, across and round and through the lives of others, towards Check-In Area D, where the queueing was to begin. I longed for wheels on my bag.

Now, here is some theory. There are professional queuers and amateur queuers. In my opinion, it is not possible for an amateur to cross the divide and 'go professional' like, say a rugby player or a football player or a teenaged fake-tanned-sequinned ballroom dancing team might do. An airport is the perfect place to prove this.

Hypothesis: Suppose that everyone in a small cordoned-off with one of those elasticated ribbon temporary barrier things area, is hoping to go in one direction, ie: towards one desk, to answer some questions and thereafter down one corridor to one plane, and suppose that some of those people arrive at eight in the morning, and find that the question-asking desk person is not yet available to ask the questions. This set of people we shall call Group A and then we can see that Group A can be divided into two subsets, A1, people who decide to stand and wait and A2 people who decide to go and get the breakfast they missed because they were rushing to get to the airport and 'I told you it wouldn't take four hours, and you never listen to a word I say'.

These, to a man and woman and hyperactive child, are amateurs.

Let us go back to the cordoned-off area which is now re-cordoned by a person who apparently is not paid to speak, into an interesting maze-formation, we see that more people have arrived and we shall call this group B. They have planned everything in meticulous detail, have used sat-nav and the AA routefinder and the TPS in-car traffic information system and Sky news and called their tour operator twice and so they know exactly that they are where they should be at the time they need to be there. They are even now, standing roughly in a line, making authoritative eye contact with Group A1 and looking slightly disapprovingly at Group A2 which is now filtering back smelling slightly of fried eggs and toothpaste. Now you may be surprised to know that every member of Group B is also an amateur. I know! I was surprised too. Until I witnessed the arrival of a representative of Group C.

By now the question-asking, suitcase-labelling, did-you-pack-this-yourself desk is open, and the maze formation area has widened, and Groups A and B are obediently filing along, and round to the left and along and round to the right and along and so on.

And about the time that I, (aspirationally in Group B but in reality I know I'm Group A1), reach the point where I am next to be dealt with, a man (almost always a man) strides round the side of the cordon, and right up to the side of a woman in a uniform with a clipboard who has miraculously appeared especially to assist him. (She will disappear equally quickly as soon as a member of Groups A or B needs her assistance).A quick word is exchanged, Oh what I would give to know what that word is, because he is directed directly to the next desk as it becomes vacant, just as I am about to move towards it. He turns, as my first foot leaves the ground, and he stares directly at my widened eyes and disbelieving mouth and he says loudly, and clearly. "You don't mind, do you, I'm in such a hurry."

Of course. He is in a hurry to get on the plane. The same plane that I, and all the other people who are standing in this agricultural livestock-farming-approved line are going to board. Eventually. When it is our turn.

And a few people behind me sigh and tut and mutter as if this is my fault!

And instead of stepping forward and shoving him violently aside with my bony elbow and speaking just as loudly and clearly right into his confident, 'I'm a winner' face, that I most certainly do mind, and then to the cheers and whoops of the assembled herd, pushing him and his expensive Asprey travel document wallet aside to replace it with my own tatty boarding card, and my bulging transparent bag of leaking foundation and nearly-finished toothpaste, instead of this, I step backwards. And then I put my case down again, and I nod, slightly apologetically, as if it would be ridiculous of me to mind at all, and I say, "Oh, no. Please, go ahead."

I defer, automatically. Because I am in the presence of a professional.

In case you are in any doubt, here are a few more examples of Group C professional queueing behaviour: 1. Pretending you didn't realize there was a queue. 2. Talking loudly on a mobile phone while walking to the front so you can pretend you didn't notice people pointing the queue out. 3. Behaving as if you own the airline, ie. Chatting animatedly to the staff, waving across to a distant desk, speaking into a Dictaphone as if it is a two-way radio.4.Speaking really loudly so people are embarrassed to be seen standing too close to you, and back away. 5. Heading for the Club Class Check-In, and apparently only realizing it at the last minute so the staff think you are being egalitarian when you step sideways (into the front of our queue) to slum it with the rest of us. And so on.

But there is some justice in the world. In these days of security-obsessed progress, no matter who you are or how professional you are, or how many people you have elbowed aside in your wake, if you want to get on a plane, you will still have to stand for at least half an hour in a draughty corridor, in your socks, with your belt and your shoes in your hand.

In everyday life, out there in the real, non-airport world, by the time a man is standing next to you in his socks with his trouser belt in his hand, you have usually progressed someway towards having sex. You have probably had dinner, and not for the first time. (I have some sense of propriety). You have had long conversations deep into the night during which you have discovered shared interests, values and information regarding your respective marital status. You may have held hands, shared a taxi. You know each other's middle names, and at some point you have decided, each of you independently, to take off your clothes together.

The dramatic familiarity of the security scanning line at an airport always takes me by surprise. Who would have thought, those socks? Those little square feet, that telltale roll of fat which, unbelted, roams freely above that waistband, the bedroomness of us all, standing there, half dressed, laden down with hand luggage as if ready to change our minds about the sex and head off to Spain at any moment.

And change our minds we do, as, breathing a sigh of relief that no forbidden item has been discovered lurking amidst our high street clothes and shoes, we scramble to put them all on again before the next person in the line follows us through the beeping archway and absent mindedly grabs our shoes, our coat, our belt.

By mid-morning, we were already near-but-not-quite bedroom partners together, in the Departures Hall. We were lighter, freed from our checked-in suitcases, scanned and approved and cleared to fly. Good heavens, we had seen each others' socks. We were almost family.

I browsed bookshops, absurd given I already had as many books in my luggage as the fiction department of a small independent bookshop, and then I browsed the beauty counters and jewellers, feeling the warmth of the pink lights, basking in the glow of the transcontinental traveller. For a minute or two I wondered if I should treat myself to a diamond bracelet because airside isn't real life. Next to me, a tall man in chinos and a button-down shirt with a sweater knotted around his shoulders, told someone on the phone that his company had diverted him to New York and he wouldn't be home for the weekend. Then he called someone else and made what sounded like a most un-businesslike arrangement for dinner at Daniel on East 65th, just off Park Avenue. He was lying and I knew he was and he knew that I knew he was. To avoid catching his eye I looked down at his shoes. Slip-on loafers.

He was a natural. And let's face it, I had become something of an expert at identifying them.

"Shall I wrap that for you, or will you be carrying it" said the assistant in the Hermes shop. I looked puzzled, and she pointed to the huge orange crocodile-skin handbag I was holding. As I considered her question I imagined the orange crocodile, jaws gaping, teeth bared ready to receive my car keys and my tissues, and peppermints and sunglasses, to consume them within his leathered depths and never let them go.

"I think I'll wait until I get back" I said. "I'd hate it to get damaged on my trip"

"Oh? The shop assistant could barely conceal her lack of interest.   "Are you going somewhere dangerous?"

"Oh yes" I said. "Very dangerous.Very dangerous indeed."

Chapter Seven : Polyester and Other Miracles of Modern Life

We are, according to the pilot, now at 40,000 thousand feet and given the high subsonic cruise rate of the 747, will be travelling at something around 570 miles an hour. (Note that I am quite the expert).The roar of the engines has dulled to a heavy hum which has insinuated itself into our bones through the logo-patterned seats so we no longer hear it, although we will still be aware of it some hours after we land.

So I shall stop dwelling on the minutiae of my past, the house, the kitchen table and the nineteen-year old husband stealer. For now at any rate. "You must free yourself from your past in order to make room for the future to flood in," said Jenna. "People spend their whole lives avoiding doing it, because they are afraid. They are afraid that when they clear the way for the future, there will be nothing there."

I imagined myself, empty, deflating like an airbed after Christmas, folding itself slowly inwards, catching old bits of paper hat and wrapping ribbon in its middle.

But not for me, the cupboard under the stairs until next year. Finally, I am turfing out the past, and waiting with faith and confidence for the future to flood in to the space I've made. I, together with 415 other people, am experiencing one of the great miracles of modern life.

It's difficult, given the thinness of the air and the soporific warmth of the cabin, the proximity of strangers and the incessant droning, to concentrate on anything for more than a minute. Beside me, Malcolm has dropped his newspaper and is gazing, unseeing into the middle distance. I am reading the laminated information sheet which I have found in the seat pocket in front of me and have deployed as a bookmark for *The Tenant of Wildfell Hall.*

This plane has a maximum take-off weight of 970,000lbs, depending on which specific model it is. I make a mental note to ask someone about the model thing but am distracted immediately by a man across the aisle requesting more of the little salty snacks which accompany our miniature drinks, and I forget what I was going to ask. Catching my eye, the stewardess smiles spookily at me and hands me two tiny little bottles of gin. Do I look like someone who needs a double? Good.

What we are doing - it's called heavier than air flight - is pretty much a product of the twentieth century. Before that, most of the flying was lighter-than-air flying, things like kites, helium and hydrogen balloons and so on. In fact, 400BC a Greek philosopher called Archytus built a steam-powered, bird-shaped machine which apparently flew 200 metres, but along came a bloke called Aulus Gellius who claimed that Archytus had cheated and used strings.

I've always been fascinated by flying. Although Louis Bleriot flew the channel in 1909, the first transatlantic air crossing, was in 1919, in an airship, which left East Lothian, flew to Long Island and then back to a military airbase called Pulham, which is in fact 29 kilometres South of Norwich, which would have been jolly inconvenient if the person who had seen you off was still waiting for you in East Lothian. A bit like flying with a budget airline which deposits you a four-hour bus ride away from the City shown as your destination, or getting out of a train at a station called Parkway, which is obviously code for 'nowhere near'.

Back to me, and us, and today. Apparently the first commercial 747 took off in 1970, and for 37 years held the record for the most people you could get onto one plane. In fact, it was designed to be modified for cargo, in case we all got sick of flying and decided to go into space, or go on the boat, or use supersonic planes, or stay at home instead. Rumour has it, that airline staff refer to passengers as self-loading cargo, but I can't believe that's true. Look at Shane for instance, and Wendy, they're smiling as if they really love us.

Wendy is the Purser, which apparently means she's the most senior of the cabin crew. Close up, she may be rather older than her high swingy blonde ponytail might suggest, and no amount of training could guarantee that exact smile for eight hours at a stretch so I suspect Botox.

Would Botox be dangerous at 35,000 feet? I think I read somewhere that silicone breast implants are prone to explode at altitude. Perhaps I made that up. I look at Wendy's serene expression as she passes up and down the aisle and imagine a green sticky toxic substance leaking from her ears as the Botox metamorphosises into an alien form and threatens to take over the plane. Whereupon I will leap out of my seat and neutralize it using small tins of ginger ale and the little plastic forks you get with airline meals, and I will be a hero.

Or, I shall just smile back at Wendy and try to work out how she ties her scarf into that clever knot which looks so casual and yet never comes undone. It's probably a whole session in stewardess training school.   Silk slithers dreadfully, so I imagine polyester is involved. Although the Queen manages it. But then, she isn't trying to serve cocktails from little cans at altitude.

The rest of the crew have introduced themselves with the intercom and cheery waves. In the First Class cabin the rich and famous are being looked after today by Pam and Gerard. We won't see Pam or Gerard, they belong to another world, and are currently handing out brushed cotton pyjamas and hanging up people's jackets. Pam is deciding which of her millionaire businessmen she will target with a view to drinks in New York this evening, followed possibly by marriage. Gerard is disappointed yet again that Sir Elton John is not on board. He dreams of meeting Sir Elton. Or Cliff Richard maybe. Every flight could be The One.

Through the curtains which lead into Club Class, we catch glimpses of Christy and Brian, who are pottering about with champagne and magazines. But back here, we have Shane and Wendy, whose every concern is apparently for our safety and comfort.

Oh Wendy. With your tight skirt, rather worn at the seat, and your polycotton shirt which gapes ever so slightly at the front, your high heels and perfect nails, is this what you wanted? You wanted to be a Blue Peter presenter too, didn't you? And instead you settled for this. High altitude servitude, accompanied by a twenty-year-old boy who is even now soliciting nightclub references from American homebound passengers. Amelia Earhart you are not.

In fact the first woman to fly was Therese Peltier, a passenger in a two-seater piloted by one Leon Delagrange in Milan in 1908. I hope she celebrated with a spot of shopping afterwards. Pottering up and down Via Della Spiga saying casually, 'I just flew here for a spot of retail therapy you know'. And probably being told off by Leon for turning up at the airport for the flight home with too much shopping, and then having to pay excess baggage charges. A bit later on in the same year, Edith Berg invented the hobble skirt when, as a passenger in a plane flown by Wilbur Wright, she became concerned that the wind would blow her skirt up over her head, and so anchored the hem with rope. Presumably she was less worried that the plane might crash and she might have to access the emergency exit in a hurry and hop away from burning wreckage with her ankles tied together.

There is a bit of controversy about the first woman to be granted a pilot's licence. The dubiously-named Raymonde Laroche claims to be the first girl to fly solo and to get the licence, but the American Harriet Quimby also lays claim to it, although she would not have enjoyed it for long, because she was flying back to Boston in 1912 with a fat passenger on board when the inequality in their weights caused the two-seater to overturn, killing them both. Even now, crew can still be offloaded if their weight creeps up a bit, and who can say that's never going to happen? If you'd spent weeks not knowing which time zone you were in, trying desperately to wake up in the morning, or get to sleep at night, or just to remember which is which, and if your boyfriend, who was a short-haul pilot turned out to be somebody else's boyfriend when you switched to long haul-duties, and your skin had dried out beyond rescue and your hair had gone frizzy, you'd be forgiven for reaching for a few comforting Danish pastries now and then.

Probably the most famous flying women were Beryl Markham and Amelia Earhart. Interestingly, they were both great society beauties, and they were also both writers, managing to capture in rapturous prose and poetry the wonder of flight. Presumably all the material available up until then consisted of technical manuals and diagrams, spattered with the oil and the blood of the generations of male aviators who had gone before.

I know this may seem unnecessarily sweeping. cruel. Later on, passionate lovers of the literature of flight will treasure the works of Antoine de Saint Exupery, Richard Bach – who could forget *Jonathan Livingston Seagull*?- Roald Dahl, and of course John Denver.

Beryl almost flew the Atlantic. In 1936 she ditched in a peat bog just a few miles short of her US destination. Personally I would have counted this as a success, in that she made landfall, but apparently it didn't count which seems harsh. So the record for the first woman to fly solo across the Atlantic went to Earhart, who did the trip in a whirl of publicity, became a celebrity and spent the whole time wishing she was in a hut somewhere writing poetry. When she vanished not long after that on a quest to fly around the world, lots of people thought she had staged her disappearance on purpose, so she could be an anonymous poet for the rest of her life without worrying about regular appearances in whatever passed for the *Hello* magazine of her day. Mind you, Beryl would have had the edge on the celebrity scoop front. She ran off with Isaak Dinesen's lover, Denys Finch Hatton. He was the one played by Robert Redford in the film, *Out of Africa*. Isaak and Beryl were good friends before that. Less so afterwards, understandably. I get that.

All those pioneers, all those campaigners, Emily Pankhurst, Germaine Greer, Ann Robinson, what did we really get? Women proved they were worth a second look, then that they might actually have a point worth listening to, occasionally. Then they proved that they could actually do things, invent things, discover things, win things. That they were ultimately, just as good as men. Or better. And now that women can do anything they want to, now we can take any job, earn any salary, run any country, travel into space, what do we do now?

Apparently, we lean across a kitchen table in Oxfordshire, full of another woman's homemade organic lasagne, our breasts spilling out of a black lacy bra, and seduce her husband, whilst pretending to be interested in his son and his golfing technique.

What did I want to do, when I was nineteen? Something. Something which would make a difference, have an effect. I wanted to change the world in some way, do something which mattered. And instead I went to art college and sat in tiered rows listening to lecturers talking about form and engineering and brush theory and Old Mastery and wrote pages and pages of notes in longhand, and tried to marshall the notes into essays and then I went to pubs and sat in cellar bars with water trickling down the walls and drank pints of beer and talked long into the night about essays and beer and lecturers, all the time only vaguely aware that none of it would make any difference at all. I wore huge sweaters and baggy jeans and for one term, a beret. And I couldn't even begin to imagine seducing Prof. Hewitt, on whom I had a monumental crush, because I was so far buried in layers of wool and self-consciousness. I didn't seduce anyone until, well in fact now I come to think about it, I've never seduced anyone.

And I don't think I've done anything which made any sort of a difference. Unlike Lucie, who at nineteen did something which made a difference alright.

At this point, I notice Wendy is leaning right over Malcolm next to me, explaining to him very patiently how to operate the seat back control. She is so close to him that if it were me, I'd want to shout 'Get the hell out of my face' and shove her violently backwards, but Malcolm seems to be enjoying it. Either that or he really doesn't know how to work the seat, which I find hard to believe.

Eventually she moves on, leaving behind a light cloud of eau-de-warm-polyester, and Malcolm turns to me. "I don't know what it is about me," he says, "they always hit on me!"

I am about to tell him that I can't imagine what it is about him either, when he carries on. "D'you know, I've lost count of the number of times a member of the cabin crew has made a pass at me."

He's obviously mastered the seat-back thing, he is virtually lying down. The woman in the seat behind him has a lap full of peanuts and tonic water.

"I was thinking about Amelia Earhart and Beryl Markham," I say to Malcolm, "and how they must have felt, being the first women to fly all alone, across the Atlantic."

"You don't mind if I get a bit of sleep now?" Malcolm says, "I've got to be at a board meeting on Madison Avenue this afternoon."

And off he goes, and here we are, Beryl, Amelia and me, all alone, half way across the Atlantic in a plane.

Chapter Eight : Beryl Triumphant

I have decided to give the honours for the first solo transatlantic flight to Beryl. After all, twenty one hours and twenty five minutes of flying in today's aircraft would have landed us on the other side of the world, and we would have had to have a stop in Singapore or Hong Kong for refuelling. And the fact that she landed in a bit of a muddle in Nova Scotia, instead of at the planned US airport is hardly reason enough to dismiss the feat. In terms of coffee places, the opportunity to purchase Duty Free Chanel No 5 and people to hold up a sign with your name misspelt on it, the lack of an official Arrivals gate may have been a disappointment, but should hardly be classed as a failure.

And anyway, I love Beryl. Born in Rutland, she moved with her family to East Africa when she was just four, whereupon her mother promptly went home again. Instead of crying for her mummy, and whining and snivelling about the heat and the insects and the lack of fishfingers, and the absence of CBeebies, she set about learning Swahili, Nandi and Masai, and by the time she was eighteen she was the first woman in Africa to get a licence to train racehorses. Inspired by an affair with a British pilot she turned to flying, and seemingly regardless for her own safety, pottered about with freight and passengers through a marriage (possibly the sole reason for which was so that she could relinquish her maiden name of Clutterbuck), and the arrival of a child, who was, by the way, only seven when she flew the Atlantic. I wonder what Greg would have said if I had come into the kitchen one morning, to find him and a seven year-old Hugo shovelling in rice krispies before the school run, only to say "You'll have to take him in today dear, I'm off to be the first woman in the world to do an incredibly dangerous thing, and I won't be back for a few days."

No wonder she was married several times. One book I read suggested she had no fewer than eight husbands. And those don't include the Duke of Gloucester, the pilot, or Karen Blixen's boyfriend, all of whom were definitely on her list of lovers. Wherever did she find the time? Greg would certainly have asked me to check whether I had washed enough shirts and bought enough groceries for the week before I even considered dallying with Royals or popping over to Long Island in a bi-plane.

Martha Gelhorn said of Beryl Markham: "Women, like men, possessed of the courage and the will, have always led their chosen lives regardless of any conventional limits." (That's in the introduction to the Virago Modern Classics Edition of Beryl's book *West with the Night* in 1984).

I suspect Ms. Gelhorn would describe me and my chosen life as having rather too much regard for conventional limits. When I was eighteen I was in love with Johnny Stokes, who was a garage mechanic. The closest I got to racehorses was when the racing was on the television before one of Johnny's beloved football matches. The closest to a plane was when we went to see a re-release of Airplane at the cinema in Oxford, and the closest I got to learning a tribal language was when I realized that, when in the pub with Johnny's mechanic mates, it was better if I didn't say anything at all.

Despite living fast, Beryl didn't die young. She was eighty three when she finally took off on her final flight, from Nairobi in 1986. I was twenty-two then, and despite the best efforts of Johnny Stokes to ruin my life, mainly by coming up with the brilliant suggestion that I get pregnant so we could get on a council house waiting list, I had managed to tear myself away from the world of the village and dreams of our own filling station, and was by then battling with the exciting new subject of contemporary art at Oxford Poly. My main concerns were sociological perspectives and sculptural techniques, losing a stone, affording highlights, and Jeffery, a politics student of some reputed promise who lived occasionally in the room across the hall from mine. Still no racehorses, still no planes, still no pioneering achievement.

If I live until I am eighty three, allowing for a bit of poetic licence, I am about half way through. Like Beryl, I have one son, and like Beryl am now making a transatlantic flight. I am risking the loss of everything that has gone before, indeed (possibly also like Beryl) I am almost welcoming the loss of everything that has gone before, and I am ready to meet whatever will greet me as I arrive on the other side. In Beryl's case, it was Nova Scotia, when she was expecting America. In mine, I daresay we shall eventually land in Newark, New Jersey, as scheduled.

I doubt I shall manage eight marriages. At the moment I have managed one, and frankly I can't really claim any credit for having managed that very well. And as to affairs? No Royals. No high profile millionaires, and to date, no husband belonging to anybody else. Of course Beryl was very beautiful. A socialite. And a poet. Would my life have been any more interesting if I had been beautiful? Are beautiful people's lives more interesting because they are beautiful? Or is interestingness in itself, a conveyor of beauty upon the interesting one? Either way, it doesn't really apply to me.

I am, effectively, standing on a bridge. Up here, in row sixty of the 747, and looking at the little picture showing the plane's progress across the map of its journey, which is on the screen in front of me, I can see that I am about halfway over the Atlantic. I am on a bridge from the past to the future, and I am half way across.

I must have spoken this last bit aloud, because Malcolm has woken up, and is looking at me very oddly. I know exactly what he is thinking, and that he is battling with the alarming and uncomfortable familiarity of waking up in very close proximity to a woman he doesn't know. All at once, he is having to adjust, as he discovers that although he has been completely asleep, and there is a woman next to him, there is no bed, there are no curtains, there is no naked shoulder to his right, no female hair spread across the pillow next to him. The air doesn't smell of his body or hers, nor of the washing powder they use, and the fabric under his face is not smooth clean cotton but some nasty synthetic stuff with little plane pictures printed onto it. Instead of her, he has me, a woman in a crushed cardigan, fully dressed, with strange bent hair and who smells of whatever I smell of, which is probably a mix of my own washing powder, and the last traces of my favourite Jo Malone's Honeysuckle and Mandarin, combined with airline fuel.

And so he must scramble up immediately, straightening his tie, pulling out the creases in his shirt, run his hands through his hair, and try to catch a surreptitious glance at himself in the reflection of his little screen to see if he has, as he fears, dribbled while he was asleep. Then he shakes out his newspaper, and refolds it to a new page, and acts as though he wasn't asleep at all. It seems he is not aware what woke him up, certainly he gives no indication of having heard my 'I am on a bridge' speech.

Thanks to a combination of boredom and gin, I am about to ask Malcolm what he was like at eighteen, when we are both distracted by the smell of overheated metal and vegetable-infused steam which fills the cabin as the meal trolley begins its journey. I calculate what meal this is supposed to be, and as it is dinner time in England and breakfast time in America, going along with my halfway theory, this must be lunch. So I ask for chicken and some white wine (Malcolm plumps for beef and the red) and find that I am really hungry.

I have never flown this far before, but even on the short flights to family holiday destinations with which I am familiar, I am always amazed by people who complain about the little things on aeroplanes. Now, a man two rows in front of me is complaining that the water for his tea isn't hot enough, and Shane is explaining that it can't be any hotter because it might spill and terribly scald someone. And another passenger is fretting because the vegetables are overcooked. Which Wendy will explain is an issue with the number of people they have to serve, and the difficulties of reheating food using steam rather than direct heat, and the passengers will sigh and roll their eyes and suggest that they could do it so much better. And I want to shout at them, "Where do you think you are? This isn't a restaurant, this isn't your kitchen, this isn't even a campsite. This is a miracle. A heavier-than-air thing, is 35,000 feet up in the air, which means that you can eat breakfast in England and lunch in America even though you have been in the air for eight hours, and you can get to another continent for around a thousand quid, and people died, so you could do this and all you care about is that your broccoli is soggy."

I don't shout of course. That would upset Malcolm, who seems to be thoroughly enjoying his beef stroganoff and has signalled for a second mini-bottle of Rioja, which cheers Wendy up no end. I wonder if she has hidden a piece of paper with her mobile number on it, somewhere in his lunch, and I really hope that if she has, he sees it before he eats it. It would be such a shame if he didn't call to ask her out for a drink later, and crueler still if it was because her number had gone the way of oversteamed broccoli and a mini-fruits-of-the-forest cheesecake, namely inside Malcolm. And, much, much later on, sitting all alone on a barstool in a downtown cocktail bar, in a non-crease wraparound jersey dress and decidedly non-airline-regulation shoes, she will look repeatedly at her watch and beat herself up over the fact that she is usually so good at spotting the ones who will turn up and the ones who won't. And she'll order another Manhattan and the barman will smile knowingly, and kindly. And she will never know that the object of her desire ate her number! Tragic.

Meanwhile I persevere with my interestingly orange chicken Provencal and my not-unpleasantly warm Chilean Sauvignon and wonder at the brilliance of it all. Beryl probably had to make do with a strip of buffalo hide and a bottle of whisky, both consumed with one hand firmly on the joystick.

A short time later, all the debris is cleared away and we are left, still belted into our little seats, with slight indigestion due to having eaten a three course meal in a very short space of time and in a very confined space, and we all look at the time, and the entertainment schedule in the seat pocket in front of us, and consider our books and magazines and wonder what the hell we're going to do for the remaining hours of the flight. All the excitement has worn off, we've done all the things there are to do, eaten all the food, drunk all the drink, and we're still only half way through. So I shall concern myself with the future.

What shall I carry with me, away from the past and into the future of me, and beyond me? What do I have from my generation that Beryl didn't have and which it is my responsibility to carry onward now that she has gone?

Twenty five or so years after Beryl Markham's death we now have:

1. The Human Genome project. 2. The Hubble Space telescope.3. Prozac. 4.The Internet. 5. Nicotine Patches. 6. DNA fingerprinting. 7.The Bagless vacuum cleaner. 8.Genetically Modified Food.9. The Channel Tunnel.10. The International Space Station.11. The Hole in the Ozone Layer. 12.The war on terrorism.13. Email. 14.The Mobile Phone. And 15.Nintendo wii.

I for one have benefited directly from 3,4,9,13 and 14, and have undoubtedly if unintentionally contributed to 11, but I can't say I actually pioneered any of them. So in real terms, I am merely a passenger in this life, and if I carry on like this, will barely deserve the little plot of land on earth in which to bury my remains, as land is increasingly at a premium and I have resulted in nothing much of any note.

Ah, you will say, but, like Jenna told you, you have Hugo. You made Hugo, and you have secured your place in future generations though him. And I shall have to say, but Beryl had Gervase. And still she made history of her own. Would Beryl have risked her life to further any one of the things on that list? I doubt the bagless vacuum cleaner would have interested her much, but yes, I believe she would. I am sure, had she been born in my generation, she would have been an astronaut.

The lights in the cabin have gone down, and most of the seats are in the recline position. Wendy leans over Roger to close the window shutter beside me, which annoys me because I like to be able to see out, even though there is nothing to see but air. From my position, trapped in this tiny space, just looking at all that air feels good. As soon as Wendy has gone, I open the blind a bit, just about an inch or so, and pile my little wad of nylon which passes for an airline pillow against it, so I can reserve the right to look at the air again later. They want us to go to sleep, and as a result, I absolutely don't want to. They can't make us. They can't make me.

Anti-ageing products which really slow down or reverse the ageing process. Cures for terminal illnesses, including, but not exclusively, cancer and Alzheimers. An ecologically sound renewable energy source. You won't need me to tell you those are pretty well beyond me. Is there anything useful I could conceivably do? Is there anything left to do here at all? Really? One thing is for sure, this is my last chance to find out.

Chapter Nine : Getting Back on the Horse

Jenna wasn't angry with Greg either. "In the end," she said, "you have to remember, he's just a man. They're children really. Put them in a toyshop and they can't resist playing with all the toys. That's why internet dating is such a disaster for the girls. No sooner has a boy found a pretty sparkly thing to play with, and as soon as he gets it home, the pretty sparkly thing lets her battery run out, or puts down her tinsel-encrusted wand for an instant, and he's back in the shop. Just browsing, he says, but he's looking just the same. And as the internet is a store in which you can just press a key and download another toy, he can hardly be blamed for continuing to shop."

Jenna was harder on Lucie. "She knew exactly what she was doing," Jenna said, "She's that type."

"What type?" I asked, wondering why if it was that obvious, I hadn't spotted it.

"You know. Spoilt. First shoes and hair slides, then a pony. Then someone's boyfriend, because you can, and because you want to demonstrate that you can. From there it's just a short skirt away from somebody's poor defenceless, bored husband who's too dumb to realise that he's been onto a pretty good thing all these years."

"Hang on!" I protested, "Greg wasn't bored."

"Of course he was darling. We all are. It's what life is like. You master the basics, eating, sleeping, walking talking, you move onto the fun stuff, maths, chemistry, art, sex, then you buy all the things, house, cars, holidays,. handbags, and then what? It's a lifelong battle against boredom frankly, and one we don't all win."

"Then you come home in the middle of an afternoon and discover your husband, who has regressed to the basics with you, is doing the fun stuff with someone else." I said.

"Exactly." Jenna had ordered a second bottle of wine at this point, as we expanded into the corner of the only wine bar for miles around. A man called Figaro pointedly left the first one empty and upended in its ice bucket on the table, to signal to any new customers how much we had drunk. We had missed lunch, and ordered tapas to cover the fact that what we wanted to do was drink wine all afternoon. When the tapas arrived, it seemed wrong somehow, as if it was inappropriate to be eating prawns *a la plancha* and *albondegas* at three thirty. Like ordering scones and jam for dinner.

"But be honest," Jenna added. "You didn't really mind. About Greg screwing that teenager. Did you?"

How did I feel? At the time? Having tried so hard to blot out the moment of discovery ever since, when she asked me the question, I struggled to remember it in detail. As I tried, I was distracted by the memory of the colour of my bathroom walls, a grey-green country pond colour, which I'd always liked, and the candles. So many of them, all lit and flickering, making shadows of the money they had cost against the tiles. The level of my bath oil, way, way down in its pretty bottle. The carpet, with its spreading damp patch where two people had sloshed about, causing little tidal waves of scented water to rush over the roll-top.

I remembered feeling cold. It was like waking up to find the duvet has fallen off your bed in the night, and for a minute you can't work out what has happened.

It was Lucie's tits which reminded me. Pretty little things, all pointy and upward, like those early little daffodils in Spring. Or maybe it was her bottom, peachy, and bigger than I might have imagined, if I had ever thought to imagine what size Lucie's bottom would be. I knew what had happened then alright.

"Actually," Jenna said, waving her glass grandly, "You should be flattered."

"Flattered?"

"That he chose a young, pretty one. Imagine if you'd got home to find that he'd got some dowdy old tart in there with him. Imagine if he preferred that to you. At least this was blindingly, depressingly, obvious."

"Would you think that? If it had been Rod? Would you?"

"I've no idea. It didn't happen to me."

Empathy, as a quality in one's friends, is somewhat underrated, I always feel.

"What you need to do," Jenna said slowly and loudly, "Is get right back on the horse."

I couldn't even remember the way to the stables. But I wonder now, if that was the point at which I began imagining some alternative sports.

Chapter Ten : The Summer of the Future

Here is a house. It's a long, low house built on split levels rather than storeys, and it sort of curves round the driveway, like welcoming arms. The front door has a pillared porch and it opens onto a huge double-height central hall. The whole house is flooded with light during the day, because on the other side, it's all floor-to-ceiling windows which look out onto the beach and after that, the sea.

In the huge open kitchen, the heart of the house, Bessie is tidying away the remains of the day's activity, cleaning surfaces until they shine and counting her blessings. Some of her friends have to manage entire families of badly-behaved people for half the money and no thanks or time off at all. Bessie works for me, and is treated as a valued member of my little family. Outside, Steve works in the garden, and during the week Lily works as my secretary and Mary arranges flowers. We're a happy crew.

Upstairs, in a 40ft bedroom with views across open country to the sea, I am getting ready for an important evening. Bessie has laid out a choice of outfits for me, but I shall take my time. I am known for getting these things right. I shall probably wear the dove grey Armani, technically understated but having great dramatic impact. And so forgiving. Not that I need it to be, I am so fortunate in my size eight figure, I am the envy of my friends, I can eat anything and never gain a pound in weight. It drives them mad!

I love these shoes. I am fortunate here too, I find my neat size five feet, inherited from my rather glamorous mother, fit comfortably into most shoes, and remarkably I have no trouble walking in heels at all, much to the delight of my dear friend Ben, who is a shoe designer and often gives me his samples straight off the runway. 'Darling, you are a better advertisement for my shoes than any amount of expensive promotion' he tells me. (Runway, by the way is what the Americans call the catwalk. And that's interesting isn't it, they name the long straight road through the buyers, celebrities and editors at a fashion show, the route which will make or break their careers, after the take-off of aircraft, the launch of journeys, the beginning of the future. The British prefer to focus on the slow, indifferent positively feline walk of the supermodel).

The shoes are more blue than grey, suede with a three inch heel, and a small jewelled 'V' shaped panel from the bridge of the foot into the toe. Despite my ability to walk confidently in the most challenging of shoes, I am glad that this evening I shall be collected by car and driven into the City. The Long island Railroad has, at last been extended, as promised, right into the heart of New York, terminating at that most wondrous of buildings, Grand Central Station, but today, even the constellations on the ceiling, the oyster bar and the delicious market which spreads into all the access subways cannot divert me from my limousine.

The dress is perfect. It will take me effortlessly from the champagne reception, to the presentation and on to dinner at Phenomenon, the latest in fine dining experiences. Phenomenon was opened six months ago by another of my dear friends, Poppy

Oliver, the precocious and exceptionally beautiful daughter of Britain's newly elected Minster for Global Responsibility, James. Poppy's food is very 'of the moment' focusing on wild plants, farmed fruit, and the most beautiful edible flowers. I love it. I also secretly, relish the fact that Poppy is English, like me, even though we are both children of the world.

Everybody is almost entirely vegetarian these days, and meat is served in tiny, teaspoon sized amounts, if at all. The planet is, we are told, benefiting from our revised diet, and the more conspicuous the consumption, the more virtuous it must be seen to be. And if I sometimes think back fondly, to an English Roast Beef lunch, or a steak sandwich with onions and mustard and....well, I just don't think back. because for the most part, Back is nothing compared with this.

Sometimes I can hardly believe I actually did it. I left the whole of the first half of my life behind, almost without a backward glance, and headed across the world to grasp the second half with both hands and make it better. Twenty years on, and I could never had imagined how much better it could be.

Of course progress does not necessarily take place in a single direction. Sometimes, progress can be sideways, or at an angle. My jeans for instance, are more 1990 than new in shape, but then again, how many versions of a trouser can there be? The new fabrics are a revelation though, advances in technology have made it possible for our clothes to adapt both to body temperature and to the outside temperature, so we no longer need layers to keep warm or dry, and a planned outfit will serve in all weathers both indoors and outside. It's terribly convenient not to have to worry about a coat, or whether you will be too hot in a sweater. Skirts are shorter than I would like at the moment, because the economy is booming, a fashion inevitability which does young girls no favours. The more champagne they can get hold of to drink, the more likely they are to end up attracting quite the wrong sort of attention. I, however, have seen it all before, and it is just so restful, not to have to go through all that, chasing, and flirting, and hair spraying and worrying, worrying, and the butterfly tummies and dreadful, sinking feelings. No, the highs and lows of life have evened out for me now, and I am entirely thankful.

For those of us who remember the first time, the second time is an opportunity to be thankful for wisdom. So now I am wise about investments, and savings, as well as about skirts and electronic gadgetry and curious cocktail mixtures. It is a great sadness though that there will be no second time for the Arctic, where now, there is never any ice, not even in the summer, or for the polar bear, a creature of the past destined to pass into legend and appearing only in children's picture books from long ago. Bears, on the whole, are much smaller now, and many people have the domestic varieties as pets. We had one for a while, although they don't live very long, so the heartbreak factor is not insignificant.

Downstairs I hear Bessie in the hall, picking up her basket and getting ready to go home. She lives about a mile away, on a small estate of about eighty weatherboarded cottages, most of which house members of the domestic staff of the surrounding county. Many of them are Bessie's relatives, her family has lived here for decades, always in service, although there are rumours that one ancestor was an Irish immigrant, who made good in the city, and built a mansion out here, only to lose it all in a card game on a wet night in a bar in Harlem. Such stories take the place of history now, we're all determined to look to the future, that's one of the things I've always loved most about America, it's what I came here for.

I don't worry about Bessie, walking home after dark. Not only is anyone with less than honourable tendencies likely to be a member of her own family, we are all tracked these days, every one of us. We have electronic devices implanted within our bodies, quite close to our hearts, and our behaviour can not only be recorded, but predicted. Of course everybody made a fuss at first, and in Europe the technology still hasn't been truly accepted, and people are forever trying to disable their trackers, or to outwit them by being eccentric, but it was ever thus, in England at least. No, on the whole, I am grateful that we can know in advance when crowds will gather and when they will turn nasty, and when a tragedy in one person's life is about to lead to history repeating itself. So the murder rate is much lower than it used to be. We are all less stressed as a result, we know this because stress is also monitored, and if you are thought to be at risk of behaving in an irrational or aggressive manner, a small memo is sent to your handset – the little device which serves as phone, and media player, information storage, diary and so on. Mine is top-of-the-range, and changes colour with my clothes, sitting quietly in my pocket like a little, hard chameleon. I rarely get a memo, although it did beep quite loudly when I began looking at an orange dressing gown in Saks Fifth Avenue. Orange is completely wrong for someone of my colouring.

I see it is almost time to leave. Looking in the mirror, I am gratified to see that I am looking pretty good for my age. The evening light is flattering, and out here it fills this room for as long as the sun is above the horizon. The Armani is lovely, one of the few 'vintage' labels still sold in the top stores. The shoes are perfect, Ben will be thrilled when I see him later.

Of course most people who have been invited this evening are younger. I am at the age when everybody is younger, but then I always felt that, even when it wasn't true. But at least my skin is clear and my hair still has plenty of bounce. For a moment, I am saddened by the knowledge that I will never grow really old, that I have only a decade left, but then surely that is better than getting tired and wrinkled and faded, or worse still losing one's mind. Now that we all know how and when we will die, and for the most part, what we will die of (accidents notwithstanding) the pressure of waking up having forgotten where you are, or finding yourself in the street in your pyjamas, or losing your keys three times in an afternoon is gone, and we no longer have to freak out about a lump, or a persistent nagging ache, or a constant headache.

No, the finalization of the human genome project has been a blessing, in my opinion. In a safe, in the sitting room of my house, is my own genome map, a thousand dollars' worth of information which has freed me from uncertainty. I will be seventy one when I die. I will not have cancer or Alzheimers, but will die because my heart will slow down, probably from the age of about sixty eight, until the point where it stops. So as we approach that point, I will have to make sure I am always wearing lovely and matching underwear in case my heart stops when I am out somewhere and I must be taken away and undressed by strangers.

I wonder if Hugo will come to my funeral. Sadly, I haven't seen Hugo since I left England. It is my one great grief. But I know, because Jenna told me, that he has a son too, and I am a grandmother. I wonder what he looks like, and what he will do with his life. His name is Icarus, which I think bodes well.

Downstairs in the big hallway, the doorbell rings. I have forgotten to tell Bessie to wait so that she can open the door, so I will have to go down myself.

George will be waiting for me. He is always waiting. He is still beautiful, even at seventy years old, and my heart skips a beat when I open the door and see him. We are not lovers, but it suits us both to let the world believe that we are. It is his limousine that we will use to go to the launch of my new book. It is already on the New York Times best seller list, and my publisher will have laid on the loveliest of everything. George relishes these events, he used to be an actor. George Clooney, his name is, you may have heard of him, If you are a woman of a certain age, like I am.

Here he is, and out I go, and in my heart I can see my grandson, high up in the sky, waving to me: hello Grandma, hello, hello hello?....."

Bother. Wendy has woken me up to find out whether I want her to wake me for breakfast before we land in New York in another couple of hours.

Chapter Eleven : The Summer of the Future : Part 2

Maybe I shouldn't try to imagine as far ahead as twenty years. I could work with the immediate future. Where will I be in a year for instance?

It's the end of a long, hard but rewarding day. I take off my working apron, fold it and place it on the sporadically operational radiator to dry. It's always pretty much wet through by the end of the day and the radiator will, in all probability, work on and off, for just long enough during the night, to dry it out. I work rose-scented handcream into my tired hands, find my coat, and turn off the lights in the shop, checking the little window at the back where the sinks are, to make sure it's locked properly. I can't imagine who would think of breaking in here, but in New York you can never be too careful. We have about eighteen dollars in the till and about a hundred buckets of flowers, but maybe a burglar in search of a cab on his way to a wedding would see it as an opportunity.

The shop is far too cold for anyone to want to sleep in it. Most people in this overheated, climate-controlled, air conditioned City can barely stand in it for long enough to choose what they want to buy. I'm used to the cold, I used to live in England. The floor is speckled concrete and chilly to the touch. There is running water, but it's always icy, and sets your teeth on edge however warm-blooded and well-fed you are. The room is like a fridge even on a hot day, due to its position, set back off a side street, with a big green awning to protect it from any sunlight. With the open air vents throwing up steam from basements, and the possibility of some solar rays during the day, the street itself is altogether a much better bet if you're planning to have a little lie down.

Of course a burglar might come in after the stock. But unless he was looking for a particularly lovely arrangement of delphiniums and cornflowers with sprays of gypsophilia and laurel to take home to his girlfriend, he wouldn't find much here to interest him.

I take a last long look round the shop as I leave, pulling down the heavy metal shutters from the outside, closing the eyelids of the building on its blue watery eyes and sending it to sleep for the night. I feel like a parent at bedtime, although the shop isn't mine. Marty, who owns it, has a chain of florists across the City, called Marty's Flowermarkets. I just run this one for him, and I'm glad of it, the money isn't great and the work is very hard on the hands but for the most part it's a happy job, and I always smell lovely, whereas if I worked in a deli or a burger joint I would smell of cheese or frying. Marty lets me take stock home too sometimes, once the flowers are in full bloom and about to droop, so my tiny flat – apartment I mean – is always full of madly coloured exotic things, dying.

The apartment is what we in England would call a studio, in that it's really only one room, with a kitchen bit at one end and a tiny shower room at the other. It's about a mile up above the street, forty stairs no less, with or without paper bags of groceries, and at every point on the stairs or in the apartment, or walking up and down the street, I feel like a film star. Probably Meg Ryan. That's what this City has done for me.

Nobody here thinks about the past. Nobody asks you, like they do in England, where are you from? Where did you go to school? What qualifications do you have? Why did you come here? Instead, they ask, What are you doing at the moment? What do you want to achieve? And whatever you say, it's cool. I'm working in a flower shop. I'm writing a novel. I'm building a house. I'm opening a theatre, I'm building a nuclear power station on the roof of my apartment, and when you answer they say 'wow! Good for you! You're going to be so good at that. And when you tell them that your shop closed, your book failed to sell, nobody came to your theatre, they say hey, these things happen, what doesn't kill you makes you stronger! And what are you going to do next? We never know what you're gonna come up with next, but we just know this is going to be the big one!

It's all nonsense of course, but it helps. When you've turned your back on half your life, left behind a perfectly good education, home, husband and child, to set up half way round the world where you know nobody and have no plans, it helps that everyone you meet tells you how sure they are that you will succeed. It certainly makes a change.

You may be wondering how, just a year on, I am working in a store – sorry, shop – without a Green Card. Well that is an interesting story, as it happens. Marty, a huge burly man I met at a 'get to know you' evening at my local bookshop (imagine that – a bookshop where they actually encourage people to come in after hours, eat , drink, read all the books and chat to everyone else) is half Brit. Not any more of course, but back then, when he was born and when he was fifteen and he worked on his father's stall at the New Covent garden market, getting up at four in the morning to make it to the market, and twice a week driving down to the docks to collect boxes and boxes of flowers. Marty fell in love with flowers but he was most definitely not in love with the early mornings, and the rain and the dark and the poor financial return for his efforts, and when he was seventeen he started getting into trouble, and hanging around with the wrong people, so one morning, just before the police arrived to pick him up for the third time that week, Marty's father gave him his passport and told him to get the hell out of the UK. Which was when Marty found out that his mother, long dead in Kensal Green cemetery, had been American.

So Marty was ideally placed to set up shop across the pond, and when he saw me at the bookshop, he recognized a fellow refugee, and somehow managed to get me a permit, on the grounds that he needed European expertise to sell the more complex arrangements his customers on the Upper East and Upper West sides required. Marty is no fool, I work much harder than anyone else in the Marty's Flowermarkets team, and unlike the others, I have to make house calls and oversee events too, to prove just how European and how invaluable I really am.

A year on and it's all worked out very well. I'm on my way home, via the fabulous foodmarket in the passageways leading to Grand Central Station, because tonight I am going to cook for a gentleman friend. Oh yes, I do have gentlemen callers, but for the time being, calling is all they do. Although this one, I feel in my heart, may turn out to be more promising, and may be allowed to make his call an overnight one. Who knows? I am free to decide, I am free to choose, I have paper bags filled with smoked ham and cheese, and fresh salad leaves, and truffle infused olive oil and chocolates, and great coffee, and I can choose. I might take a cab for the last three blocks, to prepare myself for the forty-stair mountain. I can if I want to. I am happy. That's the most extraordinary thing about all this. I work harder than I ever have before, for less money. I live in a flat smaller than bathrooms I have owned, I have nobody to call my own. I am happy.

Those of you who are still paying attention in the real world will be wondering what has happened to Hugo. How could she be happy, you will say, a year ago, she left her only son on the other side of the world. And its true.

When Hugo was born, - well about three hours after he was born, when I had stopped shaking and aching and worrying about how on Earth I was going to cope now that the world had been turned on its head, and after Greg had left and his mother had stopped wittering on about an heir for the family (An overextended semi-detached in Pangbourne, a timeshare in Malaga and about a hundred quids' worth of Premium Bonds - who did she think she was, the Duchess of Devonshire?) I looked at the baby, sleeping in the little plastic box next to my bed, and watched as his tiny body moved up and down with his breathing, and his tiny hands clenched and unclenched, and his little closed eyes fluttered, and I promised him that I would never leave him, not for a moment, not for an hour, not for a day, not for a year and certainly not for ever.

So at what point between then and now, did I start to think the unthinkable?

Maybe it was when he was ten days old, and I still hadn't had a bath or a full night's sleep, and Greg had gone to Geneva on a business trip and I wasn't sure I entirely believed him when he said he was going on his own and it was just a coincidence that his PA, Monica, was on holiday at the same time.

Maybe it was when Hugo was a year and a bit old, when Greg and I went out to dinner for our wedding anniversary and we had just got to our table at Gordon Ramsay, in Chelsea, it was the first time we had been out together since Hugo's arrival, and Greg's mother phoned the restaurant and said it was nothing to worry about but she'd noticed a rash and she was about to take him to the hospital to be on the safe side. In the end she was right about it being nothing to worry about, in fact it was nothing. I suspected her of making the whole thing up but we never went back to Gordon Ramsay.

Maybe it was when he was five, and I was told off by his primary school headmaster for taking a part time job in a solicitor's office, when I should have been at home creating a supportive parental environment.

No, it was none of these. For the first seventeen years of his life, I was utterly and happily committed to my beautiful, kind, and fundamentally ordinary, boy. I still am, of course I am. But on the day I discovered that his father had been having an affair with the girl I believed was Hugo's girlfriend, and Hugo told me it was my fault, I decided that my commitment could afford to change. Hugo had made a decision about me, without me. And so I would just have to grow up, face the music, smell the coffee, and do the same.

As I grew, faced up to the tunes and breathed in the full roast, I felt as though I was a kid on a swing, a swing which had swung happily back and forth, first very high, then rapidly through low back to very high, and back again. But as time went by, the momentum of the swing had changed, and the low took longer and longer while the high was less and less high. Until in the end, I was left, just sitting there, the swing at its lowest point, my feet barely touching the ground, hands still hopefully on the ropes, going nowhere.

Back in my future, I unpack my groceries from the taxi – yellow cabs may look romantic in films but they are one of the very few things in New York that are not a patch on the English. You can get out of a black cab in London, without having to skid across the ripped seat, stand up, reach in easily for your luggage, pay tidily through a large open window, and have a conversation about fascism, all without banging your head, being engulfed in fumes, being trapped between a seat and the bulletproof partition, blinded by a thousand information notices or being yelled at in an unintelligible dialect before being splashed to the waist with filthy effluent from the kerb by the screeching tyres of the cab in which you have just left your last bag of groceries. Presumably yellow cab drivers never have to shop for food.

I walk up the many many stairs, and despite the best efforts of a long day in a big anonymous, dirty city, my spirits are still high. I hope I will have time to unpack, change my clothes and light a few candles before my date arrives, but as I reach the last flight, I am aware that somebody is up there, on the top landing ahead of me.

Wary, because I've seen all those films too, the ones without Meg Ryan but with Jack Nicholson and Tommy Lee Jones and that bloke with the white hair that nobody can ever remember the name of, I approach more slowly, my door keys strategically woven through my right hand in case I have to punch someone in the face, I tread upwards. The first three stairs are silent, the fourth squeaks. I hold my breath. A foot moves above me, and comes to stand at the top of the stairs. I look at the foot. It is wearing a brown laced brogue which probably rules out Nicholson and Lee Jones, but leaves the unnamed albino, who has been in Bond films. I follow the shoe up the leg, which is encased in a pin striped trouser.

"Sorry. I'm terribly early" says a vaguely familiar voice, "I came straight from work. Can I help you with any of that?"

I look up at my date, who because of the three remaining stairs, is towering above me. Relief that he is not a serial killer clouds my judgement, and I smile happily. Then I see it is ...Malcolm.

How the hell did he get into this dream? It's a year since I was on that plane next to him. Did he follow me? Has he been in my life since then? How has he got here?

Wendy is back. This time, she is warning us to put our seatbelts on, because there is likely to be turbulence. You're telling me.

Chapter Twelve : Turbulence

The change in the atmosphere is subtle at first, then it sort of grows, like the noise of a car approaching on an empty road, or the spread of red wine, accidentally dropped on a pale carpet, eating up the inches, one at a time, in all directions, but also somehow losing concentration, and in an inevitable sort of way, covering everything.

It feels hotter than before, stuffier too. We're all supposed to be asleep but the rows and rows and rows of passengers, all laid out in numerical ranks, are all waking up. Even those not physically shaken into life by Wendy and her crew are subconsciously noticing the change in the ambient mood of the room, and coming back into it, curious, worried.

I can feel the debilitating stiffness in my back and shoulders, the result of sleeping awkwardly, and the fact that I have slumped sideways towards the window. It is a relief at least to work out from the pain that I haven't slumped over Malcolm, who is fiddling with his tie as if he's getting ready to address a board meeting. Perhaps he feels that if he is about to die in a plane crash, he should be properly dressed to face it.

I take *The Tenant of Wildfell Hall* out of the seat pocket again, and try to focus on the small print, although as the cabin lights are at their pre-turbulence level it is hard to see anything at all.

The plane moves oddly, it feels as though it shifts sideways, and settles again. Then it does a little rise and fall, as if over a hump-backed bridge, which makes me smile, remembering journeys of childhood in an old car, which constantly threatened us with breakdown, yet valiantly flew us over the top of small rivers and through little streams on a holiday in The Dales.

Nobody speaks. Then comes the crew announcement.

"Good afternoon" (Is it afternoon?) "Ladies and gentlemen, this is the First Officer speaking, I apologize for disturbing your sleep, but we are experiencing a bit of turbulence up ahead, a small electrical storm as we pass over the last miles of the Atlantic and approach land to the North of New York. It's nothing to worry about, just a little local quirk of the journey, but I must advise you that the seatbelt sign is now on, and therefore you are required to stay in your seats and refrain from moving about the aircraft until we get through the weather front and out the other side. I'm afraid this applies to the crew too, so unless your situation is an emergency, please also refrain from using your overhead call button. The trolley and Duty free service will be resumed as soon as it is safe to do so. I should like to remind passengers that your safety is our utmost concern, and that whilst we will do everything we can to make sure your flight is an enjoyable one, we must at times like these, defer to our safety guidelines. In the meantime, I suggest you get back to sleep if you can, and look forward to breakfast and our arrival in Newark, which is scheduled to be on time, or perhaps even a few minutes early."

So mainly, we are to refrain. An odd word, which also means Chorus, when written in a hymn book, and which presumably they would prefer us not to do. And we must stay in our seats, and try and sleep, despite the fact that we are sitting in a metal tube, 35,000 feet above the Atlantic and about to go through an electrical storm. The biggest lightning conductor for hundreds of miles in all directions, and we are all sitting, neatly in rows, inside it, waiting to be struck. Am I frightened? Yes, I probably am.

Around me, the other passengers are dividing neatly into two groups, those who are pretending not to be scared and those who are pretending to be far more scared than they really are. Malcolm falls, unsurprisingly into the first group. He is rattling his newspaper, and sighing as if this is all just too inconvenient, because he would have chosen exactly this point to get up, go to the loo, collect more papers from the overhead locker, and order some more brandy. The only real tell-tale sign is the way his right foot is jiggling up and down, which apart from being a dead giveaway, is happening right in the corner of my eye and is therefore extremely irritating. I contemplate smacking it, very hard, with *The Tenant*.

In the row in front of us, a young girl is grabbing her boyfriend's sleeve and whispering loudly about how scared she is and does he think the plane will crash? He reassures her that this is all completely normal and its all fine, but his voice gives him away. He tells her the captain has said it's all to be expected and he probably does this hundreds of times a year, but she says he would say that wouldn't he, because it's his job to make sure we don't all start screaming and running about and making the plane crash even quicker. The boyfriend doesn't seem to have much to say in the face of this brand of logic, and the girl's voice trails away on a little cloud of terror which remains above her head, and just sits there, threatening to break up and rain over her when disaster strikes.

She has made her own fear and if she expected her man to dispel it for her, she has just learnt a valuable lesson.

The plane drops suddenly. It feels like a thousand feet, it feels like being thrown off a high building while sitting in an armchair, it feels as though the ground has been taken away suddenly, but of course there is no ground beneath us, just air, and luckily, even without the thousand feet we've just lost, there is plenty more of it, and the plane settles again, In the overhead locker Duty Free bottles clink together hard and my jacket gets crushed under the new weight of someone else's bumper promotional gift box of Paco Rabanne. Somewhere, in a sort of middle distance, a child starts to cry because its ears hurt. Soon, everybody else's ears will hurt too, mainly because of the child, who will progress to piercing shrieks, but they probably won't cry because then it would look as though they are scared and they are definitely not. I mean, it's just flying isn't it? People have been doing it for decades. It's actually one of the safest ways to travel. Statistically safer than crossing the road. Oh yes.

Although right now, as the plane lurches sideways again, I think most of us would give the zebra crossing and the lollipop lady the benefit of the doubt.

There is a flash of violent light which forces its way through every tiny space between window and window blind in sudden orange stripes, whipping across our laps, and then it is gone, and then back again, and gone. You should count, says someone not far away, count between the flashes of lightning and the rumble of thunder. That tells you how far away the storm is. Nobody hears her because the rumble of thunder is right after the lightning. We are in the storm. It is no miles ahead.

It is very exciting. We are in the weather. Not looking at pictures of it, or planning for it, or even under it, we are in the weather. Right inside it, as another pair of white lightning stripes is followed by the huge rattle of thunder and the smaller rattles of plates and bolts and screws, as the aircraft is tossed about like a cocktail shaker in a cheap bar.

We are all becoming uncomfortably aware of how a plane is actually built, the seams seem to be straining, and we're sure can see the joins.

The plane drops another thousand feet and Malcolm says "Fuck!" which makes me like him slightly more. "Yes, Fuck indeed." I say. He doesn't seem to notice, but his fingers, now gripping the inflight magazine, are white at the knuckles, as he tries to pretend he will be alive to pay his next credit card bill, and proves it by trying to choose between the Duty Free MP3 player and the 'I Love New York' boxer shorts.

I can just make out Shane and Wendy, by peering through the seat backs. They are strapped into their little jump seats, cheery grins bolted onto their faces. Wendy has seemingly forgotten that the length of her skirt means she really must keep her knees together when seated opposite passengers and Shane has spilt something orange down his shirt. But still they grin and suddenly Shane laughs, as if Wendy has told a joke, which if she has, she must have done through well-gritted artificially whitened teeth.

I find I'm rather enjoying all this. I feel as though I am really on the edge of danger, am taking this huge risk, and am riding it out. This physical turbulence is altogether more satisfactory than the mental turbulence which has characterized my recent past. The ups and downs of life which at first I found refreshing, after years and years of flatness, ambling about on the level, got ugly as the months wore on and I never knew when I woke up in the morning, whether today was a rise above the clouds day or a drop out of the sky day. Whether it would be a happy time, Hugo with flowers or a job, or even a whole sentence, or whether something else would crawl out of the woodwork to destroy me, another of Greg's 'let's be honest, it hasn't worked between us for a long time' confessions, or whether another of his indiscretions would arrive on my doorstep to pierce me through the heart as I stood at the kitchen sink with a spray bottle of limescale remover.

Hell no, I reckon, as my seat drops away from my bottom in another death-defying plunge, and rises up again with equal force, ramming my shoulders up past my ears, this is none of your emotional rollercoaster, none of that being buffeted about in your own sitting room by the continuously crummy behaviour of people you've committed your life to, this is the real thing. I could die here, surrounded by strangers, gasping for air, clinging to Anne Bronte's final masterpiece and faithful to the memory of Amelia Earhart. This is something.

I must be smiling, because Malcolm is giving me a funny look.

And then, almost as suddenly as it came, the storm is gone. The plane stops screaming and reverts to its quiet but consistent hum, and the light stays constant across the cabin. A few people dare to lift the window screens and gasp in relief at the sunshine above and the level, fluffy white cloud base below. People breathe out, and smile at one another. From something that technically seems weightless, a huge multi-ton aircraft suspended in the air, a huge weight has been lifted.

There is also something new in the increasingly stale, recycled air, a sort of light bubbling sound, which we haven't heard before, It is conversation, chatter between strangers, talk, of relief, of nothing much, just the sheer joy of being alive, of being safe, of coming through a great mutual struggle and emerging the other side, united in triumph.

Wendy and Shane are positively skipping up and down the aisles now, dispensing peanuts and miniatures with gay abandon and much hilarious, some might suggest manic, laughter. Oh yes, we're all having a party now.

The captain is back.

"Hello again ladies and gentlemen," he says in his 70% dark chocolate tones, "you will have noticed that we are now safely through the worst of the weather..."

"Ha Ha!" we all laugh, "the worst of it? You mean there's more? Ha ha, funny joke..."

"....and I am reliably informed that it hasn't held us up at all, so we can still maintain our expected arrival slot on the runway at Newark. So there's no need to worry about all the grannies and granddads and long lost sisters and brothers and taxi drivers who have all put themselves out to come and meet us!..."

"Oh ha ha..." we all fall about laughing.

"In just a few more minutes, we will be flying over land once more. We will be approaching our destination over Newfoundland, and then heading down the coast over Martha's Vineyard and along the shoreline until we hit New York. ..."

"Not literally!" I hear someone shout, and we all collapse with mirth.

"...As you can see, I've switched off the seatbelt light, so if you wish you may move around the cabin, and then I suggest you all just sit back, avail yourself of the in-flight entertainment we have on offer, and enjoy the rest of your flight."

So everybody gets up and shakes themselves down, and people start crashing up and down the aisles and opening the lockers to make sure nothing is broken or spilt and things inevitably have been dislodged and therefore fall out and injure those underneath, and for the most part, everyone is fine about it, because although we may have been hit quite hard by a falling litre of Johnnie Walker at least we aren't dead or fighting our way out of burning wreckage only to be consumed by frostbite or polar bears or sharks, or harpooned by a whaling fleet.

The couple in front is kissing with relief. Well if I'm honest it's rather more than relief. Gusto would be a better word. Come to think of it, it's rather more than kissing. Through the gap in the seats I try not to fix my gaze on his hands travelling clumsily around her body. Propping *The Tenant of Wildfell Hall* in the gap I can only hope that Helen Graham's moral compass by a process of osmosis, is useful to him.

Would anybody have missed me? Really?

For a while there, I thought that I might never get to New York. That I might never have the second half of my life, that the first half was in fact, the whole thing. And that if it was, I had lived it without knowing, that that was all there would be and as a result had in fact wasted it.

I know. There is Hugo. But then if I was to die in a horrific air tragedy when he was just nineteen, might it have been better if neither of us had ever been there at all?

No. Of course not. Hugo is better for having been in existence, for all of his near twenty years, in all his solid, clumsy, dirty blonde and slightly smelly glory. And if the world is better for having him in it, it must therefore go without saying that the world is better for having had me in it. Phew. And Greg, Less phew, but phew just the same. At least we did something right. Ish.

But that still leaves me as being merely a conduit to providing the world with Hugo. Is that enough?

Jenna says that we are all just passing through, that Earth is only a single point on a much longer journey, which makes me think of it as a fare stage on a sort of inter-galactic bus route, but being so much more spiritual than I am, she has a much more beautiful view of it all. Our work here is important, of course it is, she says, but it is incidental in the scheme of things.

That makes me think of those Sisco Wall charts, where schemes and things are drawn and pasted onto vinyl in DayGlo colours, where critical paths through the Great Year of Life are annotated with stick-on stars for good behaviour, and other people's frantic claims on two-week sections of July and August leave you with depressing low-season holiday options.

I get no stars for leaving Hugo. Who is probably even now, lying on the sofa, his trainered feet on the coffee table, next to last night's takeaway boxes and empty beer cans, and watching Bargain Hunt, believing it to be career enhancing because it looks like a way to make money without leaving the house. He probably hasn't noticed I've gone yet. I gave up clearing up after him when I realized that he didn't care either way. Actually that's not true. I gave up clearing up after him when he said it was my fault that his girlfriend had an affair with his father.

Either that, or Greg has found my letter, propped up on the dresser in the kitchen beside the teapot (very Alan Bennett), and has sat him down for one of their ludicrous man-to-man chats, where Greg says 'man-to-man' a lot, and Hugo says, 'Yeah Fine Dad, Whatever'.

The teapot? What was I thinking? That letter will be there forever. That was about as pointless as leaving it on the lid of the loo, or sellotaping it to the nozzle of the Hoover. Oh well.

Jenna. Now Jenna would miss me. Although she would probably see my death in the 2014 Boeing Air Disaster as some kind of sign that she should go off on her bike again and ride round Belgium to find solace, or that she should make a massive donation of all her worldly goods to a bearded guru in Nevada. The last time she did that her worldly goods were returned to her by the Las Vegas police department; she couldn't hope to be so lucky a second time. But I think she would miss our long rambling philosophical talks, and our mutual discovery of art and music and wine, our almost entirely fictional accounts of sexual conquests, and our shared love of the idea of sisterhood, although the reality had always been a bit beyond us.

Seven would be sad if I died. The very thought of that makes a little burn mark on my heart. Just there. Right now. Like very hot tea which has gone down the wrong way. Lovely little girl, with all her feelings in the right place at the right time. How did we all manage that between us, Jenna, Rod, Seven's would-be rock-musician-and sometime-financial-adviser father, me, her permanently angry and usually vague godmother, Hugo, her grubby and occasionally kind boy next door, however did we all manage to make someone so utterly, wonderfully normal ?

No, for Seven's sake I'm thrilled I didn't plunge into the Atlantic with Malcolm and Wendy and Shane and Captain Carlton.

And I would never have made it to the airport in New York, where somebody may – or may not – be waiting for me, and I would never have known whether he was there or not. I would never have met Marty or worked at the flowermarket, and I would never have written a heap of best selling books, and I would never have shopped at Grand Central, or eaten at Daniel, or owned the weatherboarded house on Long Island, and I would never have grown up to be the grandmother of a child called Icarus and to be the regular date of actor George Clooney.

Well done me, for having made it through the storm.

I hear a new sound, a sort of deep but wavering rumbling, louder then softer, rising and falling, a sort of baritone chant. I realize that Malcolm is speaking to me.

"You're obviously a frequent flier," he says.

"What makes you say that?" I ask, although I'm pleased. It's the impression I've been trying to create.

"You seemed to be very calm. When it all got a bit rough back there."

Malcolm is American. I hadn't factored this into the equation at all. I had just assumed he was English, on his way out to a business trip, that his home was in somewhere like Basildon, and that, unlike me, after a few days in New York he would just get back on this plane and fly home again.

"Oh, nothing much bothers me," I say, although somehow the idea that he might be my new neighbour does.

"Are you going on holiday?" he asks.

I am affronted. I've tried rather hard to look like a seasoned traveller. After half a life spent doing only things which could reasonably be expected of me, I am for the first time doing something dramatic, unpredictable and well actually incredibly brave, and apparently, even now, I look like an ordinary middle-aged woman on a weekend mini-break.

"No, No," I assure him in what I hope is an 'amused by your silly typical assumption' kind of voice, "I'm going home actually."

Malcolm puts aside his rather tattered newspaper and turned as far as was humanly possible in a very tight space wound round by a fastened seat belt, towards me.

"You live in New York? Which part of the City?" he says, surprised.

I consult my memory of the *Rough Guide to New York*.

"Oh, the Village," I say. I love the sound of The Village. Would Marty's Flowermarket be in the Village?

I know, Marty doesn't exist, except in my orange-chicken-infused dream, and there is no Flowermarket, but there could be. I believe in it. I believe in Marty, and his dying, demanding mother, and his passion for tulips in Spring and the way he always cries when he makes up wedding bouquets and he always laughs when he does funeral wreaths. "Weddings," he says, "so much hope, so little chance of success," and, "Funerals, so much money on flowers and they'll all forget him in a week."

"The Village?" says Malcolm, "Me too! East or West?"

"Um..." I say, trying to remember what I've read. East, mainly hippies, yuppies and immigrants, bohemian, eccentric, poorer, West is smarter, fashionable, expensive, the Village of movies and television. Which one would I live in? "Well, the middle really," I say eventually.

"Greenwich?" says Malcolm cheerfully. "I live on the corner of Morton and Washington. There's a great little deli there – Philly's – do you know it?"

"Of course," I say confidently. "I love Philly. She's one of my best friends."

"Really?" says Malcolm, sounding surprised. "I thought Philly was after Philadelphia. Where Rob and Joe ,who run it, come from. Funny that, I never knew Philly was actually a person."

"Oh yes." I say, confidently.

"So you probably hang out in Washington Square?"

"Every Sunday."

"I'm amazed we've never run into one another. I walk Barney at the dog patch in the Square on Sundays! Well, I must make a point of looking out for you!"

I think about this for a moment. It is suddenly very tempting, to capture a future event, to hold in my head, a place to be, a time, a real person. I could write it in my diary, my first proper engagement, on landing: Sun pm: Malcolm, Washington Square Dog Patch. "Absolutely!" I say.

"We could grab a coffee at St Marks' Place."

"Oh I love to do that."

"Are you on best friend terms with St Mark too?"

"Ha ha! You're funny. I love the atmosphere, the way it's so totally West Side."

"Except that St Mark's Place is in the East Village."

Bugger.

"Yes. but I always think it has such a West - ish vibe, don't you?"

There is a bit of a silence.

"So," says Malcolm eventually, "You don't really live in the Village do you?"

There is a bit more silence, while I try to work out what to do next.

"Not yet," I tell him. "I'm going to. That's where I'm going. This is a one way ticket."

I wave my ticket at him.

"It's a return," he says, looking at it.

"I know," I tell him, "They wouldn't sell me a one-way. But I'm not planning to go back. I've left England for good."

Malcolm raises an eyebrow. "I won't ask," he says. People often say that when they expect you to tell them something without them asking.

I think quickly. There are about 20 million people living in New York. The City is 47-odd thousand square miles and what with parks and so on, and the teeming traffic, the chances of my bumping into the one other person I know at any point in the next ten years is...well one in... it's remote.

"The truth is, I had to leave." I say.

Malcolm turns even further round in his seat. I fear for the impossibility of his ever being able to turn back, and wonder if he will suffer terrible damage to his internal organs.

"Had to? Are you on the run?" he says, "How interesting! You do know that convicted criminals aren't allowed to enter the US? People with a history of mental illness, anyone who has been declared an enemy of America are prohibited. Oh, and people who have been on a farm have to work a bit harder to get in too."

"Not that sort of had to," I say hurriedly. "I just had to get away. I'm not a murderer. Honestly. I've never wanted to harm anyone. Well not properly harm them, not well, not stab them or strangle them or throw them off a cliff or anything."

I sound like a murderer. Or a madwoman. Perhaps I should just own up to my trip to the Valley Forge Farm Shop last weekend and have done with it. Might as well be hanged for a sheep poo and a rack of lamb as for illegal immigration.

"Like I said, I won't ask." says Malcolm. There he goes again, asking.

"What about your husband?" he asks next.

"I'm not married," I say

"Yes you are." he says.

"Not any more," I say, and as I say it I wave my hand vaguely and notice my wedding and engagement rings. Wrenching them off I hurt myself really quite badly.

"Can't think why I've still got them on," I say airily.

"Probably to fend off the unwanted attention of strange men." says Malcolm. "Very sensible. Anything could happen."

"Oh yes. That was it," I answer, dropping the rings into the pocket of my cardigan. I tell myself that the slight unease I feel   is because my engagement ring is an antique ruby and worth quite a lot of money, rather than because my left hand is now bare after twenty-odd years of being rather well dressed. We both ignore the little band of white raw-looking skin where the rings were.

"Big decision." says Malcolm.

I suppose it's the relief that we weren't killed that has brought us so close together. I find myself telling Malcolm about Greg and the child Lucie. When I get to the bit about finding them in the bath and being upset about my expensive bath oil, Malcolm positively guffaws, which I find a bit insensitive.

Wendy is over like a flash, her nylon legs cracking with the static of sudden movement.

"Are you alright?" she says caringly to Malcolm, stroking his arm, "Can I get you anything?"

Malcolm has tears pouring down his cheeks and I have a feeling they aren't tears of sadness for the wrongs I have been done.

"I'll have a brandy," I say, firmly. Wendy looks up as if she has been interrupted during a complicated operation to save the life of a dying child.

"What?" she says, really quite rudely.

"She'll have a brandy," Malcolm says. "And so will I."

Wendy is almost as red as her uniform. If anything not made of nuclear waste could be quite that shade.

"Fine," she says, stalking off. Malcolm looks at me. "Oh dear," he says. "I think you may have inadvertently dashed some hopes."

"I shouldn't worry about it," I say, "There are another fifty rows behind us, I'm sure she'll find someone to love her. It was probably just the suit that attracted her. Or the shoes. Or just the fact that you're a man." I hope he doesn't think it's significant that I've noticed his suit or his shoes.

"Actually, I'm a bit shabby these days," he says. "That's what happens when you jack in your job on Wall Street to become a gardener."

Interesting.

"You don't look like a gardener," I point out. "It may be shabby, well I don't mean that... well what I mean is, gardeners don't usually wear suits at all. They wear trousers,. Corduroy. That's needlecord to you I think. You know, the little lines, green or brown mainly, although it does come in red. And yellow. Anyway, gardeners usually wear, well, gardening clothes...." I am babbling like a pan of potatoes left on the stove. A moment more and I shall break down completely, and all I will be good for is mash.

Malcolm laughs again. It is a quite a nice laugh, sort of comfortable and kind. Can a laugh be kind?

"I'm not actually a gardener," he explains. "I run a company of gardeners. We buy up little plots of land all over the city, with donations made by rich people, and turn them into little gardens for poor and homeless people to sit in."

"Wow." I say after a long while. "That's a really good thing to do."

"It beats making millions of dollars a year, eating in the world's best restaurants, holidaying in Bermuda, shopping at Bloomingdales and sailing my own boat off the Hamptons at weekends."

"Does it?" I say, because of course it doesn't.

"Now I don't earn anything, I live off the last decent investment I made before giving up the money business. I eat at hot dog stands, holiday in Central Park, the only shopping I do is at the deli, and if I want to go sailing I take the Staten Island Ferry."

"Why?" I say stupidly.

"It's free, and it's one of New York's best attractions. You should try it."

"No, not why the ferry. Why did you give up all that, to have nothing?"

"Well, I got to where I had always wanted to be, and when I got there I couldn't remember why I wanted to be there. I decided it wasn't worth the chase. And I got to fifty and I thought I'm half way through my life and I want the second half to be different."

"Snap," I say, "Well, not the bit about giving up a million dollar job to do a good thing for poor people, obviously. But snap about the bit where you decide to make the second half of your life different from the first half. It's cool. That's what my son would say."

"You have a son? Do you have a picture?"

I show him the little picture of Hugo I carry in my purse. It was taken on a holiday in Wales, so it's raining. He is standing on a little bridge, wearing an anorak with the hood up, but you can still see his yellow hair, and he has his hands in his pockets and he is scowling because he is cold and wet and he hates having his picture taken. But you can still see the blue of his eyes, and the funny little dimple he has on only one side, and it is so utterly exactly like him, that it's the one I always look at, when I want to find my son. A smiling one would be very strange and probably quite scary.

"Here," says Malcolm, pulling out his wallet. "That's Barney."

"Fine," she says, stalking off. Malcolm looks at me. "Oh dear," he says. "I think you may have inadvertently dashed some hopes."

"I shouldn't worry about it," I say, "There are another fifty rows behind us, I'm sure she'll find someone to love her. It was probably just the suit that attracted her. Or the shoes. Or just the fact that you're a man." I hope he doesn't think it's significant that I've noticed his suit or his shoes.

"Actually, I'm a bit shabby these days," he says. "That's what happens when you jack in your job on Wall Street to become a gardener."

Interesting.

"You don't look like a gardener," I point out. "It may be shabby, well I don't mean that... well what I mean is, gardeners don't usually wear suits at all. They wear trousers,. Corduroy. That's needlecord to you I think. You know, the little lines, green or brown mainly, although it does come in red. And yellow. Anyway, gardeners usually wear, well, gardening clothes...." I am babbling like a pan of potatoes left on the stove. A moment more and I shall break down completely, and all I will be good for is mash.

Malcolm laughs again. It is a quite a nice laugh, sort of comfortable and kind. Can a laugh be kind?

"I'm not actually a gardener," he explains. "I run a company of gardeners. We buy up little plots of land all over the city, with donations made by rich people, and turn them into little gardens for poor and homeless people to sit in."

"Wow." I say after a long while. "That's a really good thing to do."

"It beats making millions of dollars a year, eating in the world's best restaurants, holidaying in Bermuda, shopping at Bloomingdales and sailing my own boat off the Hamptons at weekends."

"Does it?" I say, because of course it doesn't.

"Now I don't earn anything, I live off the last decent investment I made before giving up the money business. I eat at hot dog stands, holiday in Central Park, the only shopping I do is at the deli, and if I want to go sailing I take the Staten Island Ferry."

"Why?" I say stupidly.

"It's free, and it's one of New York's best attractions. You should try it."

"No, not why the ferry. Why did you give up all that, to have nothing?"

"Well, I got to where I had always wanted to be, and when I got there I couldn't remember why I wanted to be there. I decided it wasn't worth the chase. And I got to fifty and I thought I'm half way through my life and I want the second half to be different."

"Snap," I say, "Well, not the bit about giving up a million dollar job to do a good thing for poor people, obviously. But snap about the bit where you decide to make the second half of your life different from the first half. It's cool. That's what my son would say."

"You have a son? Do you have a picture?"

I show him the little picture of Hugo I carry in my purse. It was taken on a holiday in Wales, so it's raining. He is standing on a little bridge, wearing an anorak with the hood up, but you can still see his yellow hair, and he has his hands in his pockets and he is scowling because he is cold and wet and he hates having his picture taken. But you can still see the blue of his eyes, and the funny little dimple he has on only one side, and it is so utterly exactly like him, that it's the one I always look at, when I want to find my son. A smiling one would be very strange and probably quite scary.

"Here," says Malcolm, pulling out his wallet. "That's Barney."

I'd forgotten the Sunday afternoons, so I was slightly taken aback to be confronted by a huge long-haired golden retriever with a red spotted bandana round its neck. "He's my baby," says Malcolm.

"Great! I suppose he keeps you on your toes," I say cheerfully, although I have always been rather wary of people who talk about animals as if they were children.

"He does indeed," says Malcolm. "Well that's us! Now what shall we do?"

I think to myself, no wife? no children? And I look at him, Capability Brown in pin stripes, and I decide, What the Hell.

"Let's have another drink," I say. "And tell each other secrets."

Wendy sends Shane along the aisle with the drinks. Shane looks almost as disappointed as Wendy was at Malcolm's lack of interest. "You start," I say.

Malcolm looks at me earnestly, thinking.

"I am afraid of zips," he says eventually.

I raise my eyebrows.

"Yup," he continues. "I have to get someone to help me with...."

"Trousers?" I say.

"Suitcases. My trousers are all button fly."

Oh God, I've actually looked. You can't help it can you? Especially when someone says 'trousers'.

"Oh. Right. Must be inconvenient." I am waving my hands about and I have no idea why. I am looking up, up at the little row of call buttons and wondering if there's one which can make me disappear without trace.

"You get round it." He doesn't seem to have noticed. "Your turn," he says.

I think for a minute. "I buy cakes and desserts and pretend they are my own."

"Is that important? Is it often necessary for you to provide cake?"

"Weekends at home. School bakery sales, birthdays, Christmas."

"That doesn't sound like too much of a crime."

"Friends used to ask me to make their birthday cakes, because I was so good at it."

"Well you're good at shopping for cake, that's almost the same."

"I did a wedding cake."

"They thought you'd baked it yourself?"

"They gave me a lovely present for doing it."

"Gee. You must buy a mean cake."

"Your turn."

"I stole my dog."

"What? That's terrible! That's much worse than passing off cake!"

"I was on vacation, in Baltimore. I was passing a truck stop and I saw him, tied up by a rusted old trailer. He looked miserable and thin and neglected and so I waited until it got dark and nobody came to look after him or give him any food or water, so I stole him."

"Well it sounds to me like you rescued him. That's a good secret. Where is Baltimore?"

"Rescue, theft, theft rescue, it's a technicality. I'm not sure I'd get off."

"If you ever go to jail for grand theft canine, I'll come and visit. Unless Baltimore has the death penalty? Anyway, I forgive you."

"Your turn again."

The brandy, the altitude, the lack of oxygen, the long hours of sitting still started to take effect. Well that's my excuse.

"I've always wondered about joining the Mile High Club," I said.

There was a bit of a silence.

"Really?" said Malcolm. "Would you consider it?" It seemed like a general enquiry rather than an invitation. But I couldn't be sure.

"I don't know. I might. I've always wondered about it. Although I'm not entirely sure I know what it is. I mean I know it's sex on a plane, but...."

"You know what? Me too."

"Really?"

"I mean, for a start, this plane is at least 35,000 feet in the air. Which is somewhere in the region of seven miles. But they don't call it the six and a half mile high club, do they?"

"No. And isn't it supposed to be about the loos? Isn't that where you're supposed to go to do it- join, as it were?"

"You mean the bathroom. I believe so."

"But everyone would see you go in there. Together. And anyway, there's a permanent queue."

"Perhaps you don't care about that. If you're keen on membership."

"And that space, it's very small. There isn't really room for one person to do what the facility is designed for, let alone for two to do something else entirely."

"You're a very practical woman, aren't you?"

Malcolm was looking right at me. I didn't want to be a very practical woman. I was on the edge of yet another precipice, staring at danger. But which way did the danger lie? In doing something, or in not doing something?

It was becoming apparent to me, that a mantra of 'you only regret the things you don't do', might not be as reliable as I had thought. I did a quick count. Things I did, that I regret. Things I didn't do that I regret. Before many seconds had passed, there were plenty on both sides.

When it comes to sex, it seems we're all wired a bit differently. Certainly when it comes to caring about whether we do it or not. Several times in my youth I found myself struggling not to do it because I felt I shouldn't for some reason and afterwards wondered why I'd bothered to defend myself from something it seemed I wanted. Whereas Jenna just went ahead if she felt like it. And so it seemed, did Greg, even when he had a pretty solid reason why he shouldn't.

If I had sex with Malcolm, a complete stranger, right now, in this plane, nobody would ever know. He didn't know anyone I knew, so there would be nobody to tell and nobody I knew would ever find out.

Then again, I am still me. Someone who, on the whole, doesn't have sex with people she has only just met. If I went ahead with it, would I still be me?

I think if you have sex with someone, you might just be bound to them in some way, for ever. Perhaps that's why they call it the mile-high club. As if its members are linked, across the globe. I picture the potential reunions, coachloads of seventy year olds meeting at motorway service stations. They would choose motorway service stations because that's the point, just getting together, whilst being nowhere in particular.

Oh hell. Does it matter? Really?

I panicked.

"I have another secret," I said.

"Go on," said Malcolm. I got the feeling he was laughing at me.

"It might not be relevant."

"It might be highly relevant."

"I'm terribly claustrophobic," I said. "And I'm very allergic to stainless steel."

"Really?"

"Oh yes. One touch of bare skin on stainless steel and I have to be hospitalized."

"Well, that wouldn't do at all," said Malcolm. There was a short pause. "Best leave it then," he added.

We sat in companionable silence for a while. The plane bobbed and whistled calmly, and on the screen in front of us, the oversized plane icon made its way along the thick dotted line across the sea.

Wendy wheeled the Duty Free trolley down the aisle, dispensing sunglasses and perfume and furry headphones. People shopped, while I contemplated whether I had just averted a disaster or missed an opportunity. Wendy didn't even look at me as she offered litres of gin.

Duty Free. No duty. The concept applies where you are not, officially anywhere, so duty cannot be assigned. If it happens nowhere, does it happen at all? Is an affair in the sky even real?

Chapter Thirteen : Traitors to the Cause

I first went on an aeroplane when I was six. I flew to see some relatives, from one end of England to Scotland, all by myself, with a big sticky 'Unaccompanied Minor' label on my chest. I loved it, and everything about it, from the excitement of being in the air to the airport, where I remained Unaccompanied for longer than anticipated as the relative collecting me had been told the flight was cancelled due to fog and had gone home. I sat in the meteorological tower and ate jelly babies and chatted happily, or so I'm told.

From then on, I had always associated flying with being independent, successful, and happy. Sadly, I didn't do much more of it, journeys being restricted to annual holidays, and even then. it was a matter of dreadful charter flights where we were herded like cows and within minutes of arriving at the departure airport were desperate for it all to be over. I ruined one notable week in Majorca dreading the flight home.

The thing is, I've always known that I didn't really belong anywhere. That's why planes suit me, I'm happy when I'm not technically anywhere. Motorway service stations count too, but they aren't as exciting, although there is more to do. When people ask me, where are you from? I don't know the answer. When they say again, patiently, where do you think of as home? I can't answer that either.

I can answer with the address of my house, I can tell you which hospital I was born in, but I don't have a clue about Home.

Looking back on it all now, wearing the mellowing, sepia-tinted glasses of hindsight, I think I was always looking for somewhere to call home, only in those days I mistook people for places. My first love was Donny Osmond, but only because he smiled all the time and had a huge family. I wanted to be on that ranch, or round that big table, or 'on the road', with all those people who loved him, and I wanted them to love me too. I had a dream once, in which Mom Osmond and the older Osmond boys told me that I was the best thing ever to happen to Donny.

And after that phase passed, due mainly to lack of an opportunity to get to Salt Lake City in Utah, and the fact that Laura Goldsmith in my class declared that Donny was in love with her (over which I had to admit defeat, she was much prettier than I was and she'd actually been to an Osmonds concert) I fell in love with my maths teacher. He was called Mr Gordon, and he had red hair and wore a brown zip-up cardigan. Mr Gordon was a family man, I loved the way he talked to us about his children and his wife and how he did DIY around the house at weekends. I didn't want Mr Gordon to leave Mrs Gordon for me, I just wanted him to need me around, which sadly did nothing for my ability to understand trigonometry.

Then we came to my first real love, by which I mean love for a real person. That was after Johnny Stokes, and before college Jeffery. His name was Rob Carter and he lived next door but one. Rob wasn't a catch exactly, but he was a year older than me, and he had his share of female admirers. But he seemed to like having me around. And his mum really liked him having me around because it meant he wasn't in the pub or riding round the village on his motorbike, or hanging about with bad girls. "The trouble with some girls," she would say, "Not that I'm saying any of them are bad people, but some girls they just decide what they want and then they'll stop at nothing to get it."

I had no idea what she was talking about. It seemed to me to be a bit unlikely that her Rob would have anything that a bad girl would stop at nothing to get, but there you are. He was kind to me and we went out for walks and held hands and once we went to see Superman at the cinema and he said he'd always come and rescue me if I was ever falling off a building. Which was lovely, but after that I started to mind if I didn't know when I was going to see him again, and I started to worry if I saw him with anyone else, even if it was a teacher or Brian Downey, his best mate, and I started to feel it all, really really deeply, which was very time consuming and sad.

I think that was when I became aware that love is actually very uncomfortable and a bit of a nuisance, in that it dictates your whole life. One way or another. It's agony when you're in it, and you wish you were free. And you really believe that you would be fine if you were free, and you could be who you were supposed to be, and do all the things you want to do and achieve your true Potential. Then he dumps you and you don't come out of your bedroom for a week and all you can do is cry and draw his name on your pencilcase, and read his horoscope in all the papers until you find one which says 'You will realize you have made a big mistake, but it's not too late to put it right' or something similar. And after about a month or two, you start to think it might be nice to be in love again, because for some inexplicable reason, you have completely forgotten how horrible it was.

And you know what, you never, never grow out of it. Even here, up in this plane, seven miles high, with all the loves of my life back there, behind me and down on the ground, I am still susceptible to it.

Right now, I wonder if he will be there to meet me. I wonder if he's The One, or at the very least, the next one. I wonder what it would be like to live as someone who is in love with an American. To walk in Washington Square, have coffee at St Mark's Place, choose pastrami on rye at Philly's, with a lover. I am free to be in love, and so by definition, I am not free at all.

Would we choose to be without the whole thing we call 'in love'? Would just 'love' do? Love for each other, our parents, our children. Would there then be room for love for ourselves, and even love for a Cause?

Emmeline Pankhurst had a husband and five children. Her husband was very supportive of her apparently, but even so, and perhaps because of the whole school-run, games kit, PTA meetings thing, she didn't really get going on the 'doing not saying' bit of her campaign until after he had died, and she was forty.

Joan of Arc was a French peasant girl who managed to fit in leading a revolution before being burnt at the stake at the age of nineteen. If she managed to fit in a twilight hand-holding walk in a rural apple orchard I'd be surprised, never mind a full blown love affair, with all its turning up on freezing football touchlines, practicing your married signature, and worrying continuously about the prospect of being dumped for Marie of Anjou or Susan of Reims.

And Florence Nightingale turned down a more than adequate offer of marriage from a Baron, no less, who was also a politician and a poet (clever, romantic and literate – sounds pretty good from where I'm sitting). She did this because she believed marriage would interfere with her vocation. She hung out with a few chaps after that but she didn't let any of them get in her way. No weeping or wringing of hands for her, she was far too committed to soothing and wringing out of bandages, and revolutionizing the care of the war wounded. Would she have been swayed by a Crimean Donny Osmond? Did she pine, secretly, for a dashing doctor or a super surgeon? I shouldn't think so, because if she had, she would never have been free to commit herself totally to her work.

Which, I suspect, is why the rest of us are traitors to our cause, and why so many of us are not Joan of Arc, or Florence Nightingale, or Emmeline Pankhurst. And why for most of us, our best defences against prejudice, unfairness, life without a man and the lack of a cure for cancer, are dresses and shoes and make up and chocolate.

Chapter Fourteen : Sad Songs

What is the saddest song ever written? The contenders are: *Is that all there is*? by Peggy Lee? *Without You*, (Harry Nilsson) Marianne Faithfull's *The Ballad of Lucy Jordan*. That poor woman (Lucy Jordan, not Marianne Faithfull). There are entire websites dedicated to finding the world's saddest song. But no. For me, it's *By The Time I get to Phoenix*. A man is leaving a woman and charts his progress on the journey by imagining what she'll be doing as he gets to various places along the way. I have to say her life sounds pretty mundane, so if it was excitement he was looking for, I'd say he'd started off with the wrong girl. Seemingly he agrees with me, and as he potters on through Albuquerque, Oklahoma, Phoenix, all those poetic sounding places, she's mainly sleeping, working and crying. At no point is she ringing round her friends to rally support, drowning her sorrows in whisky or Chardonnay in a bar, throwing his remaining possessions out of an upstairs window, or eating a family sized bucket of ice cream whilst watching *Bridget Jones' Diary* on DVD. I'd say Jimmy Webb (the man who wrote the song) hadn't actually asked any women what they would do in the circumstances.

Phoenix, Albuquerque, Oklahoma, where is he going? If he continues in a straight line, he'll eventually hit the East Coast around Charlotte, having dropped in on Atlanta, home of Coca Cola, CNN and, according to a strange business trip where I once tagged along with Greg, the most fried sugary food I have ever seen on a single plate. So he'll be feeling a bit sick and a bit fatter, and will be an expert on the history of Coca Cola, and when he arrives in Charlotte, what will he do? After spending time at the Discovery Centre, and hanging out with the kids in a huge number of nightlife venues, and a bit of rollerblading, he might check out the NASCAR events, and then, what?

Was it worth leaving her for? Really?

You see what I am getting at. He's travelled the whole width of the USA, and she's cried and worked and slept and presumably come to terms with the fact that he's finally left her, and gone out to the supermarket to buy the ice cream, where she has met a very nice man in aisle twenty seven (cereals and rice) whose wife has died, and currently they're getting on very well, and are thinking of moving in together. Meanwhile, he has had three girlfriends in succession all of whom were substantially younger than he is, (what do you expect when you hang out at the Discovery Centre and the rollerblade hire shop), and he's living over a drive-in McDonald's and wondering where his life went. And suddenly, on a whim, late one night and after half a bottle of Jack Daniels, he decides to ring the Left Woman, and the phone just goes on ringin' 'Off the Wall'. Sound familiar?

Well I'm not going to spend too much time wondering what Greg is doing. I've been gone since yesterday lunchtime, so I imagine he's wondered vaguely where I am, unless he's found the letter (see the earlier bit on how unlikely that is) in which case he still won't know where I am but will know that it's on purpose, and I haven't just got waylaid at the supermarket, or gone to find Jenna, or been kidnapped by aliens. And rather than crying, I expect he and Hugo went out and ate Bad Food.

I was about twenty one, when waiting for life to begin was replaced by waiting for it to get better. Greg had left university a year or so ahead of me, and he was already a Chartered Surveyor. I've never really known what a Chartered Surveyor does, and whenever I've asked I've always ended up with a description of an architect, or a town planner, so I'm none the wiser. However it did mean that Greg, unlike any of my previous boyfriends, had disposable income which stretched further than eight pints of beer and a kebab on the way home. And he was very good looking, at least I thought so. Jenna called him the Anchorman, because she said he looked like an American television newsreader, all square jaw and short back and sides, with the occasional coloured tie, demonstrating his inner eccentric. He was quite good at sex too, I seem to remember, although I'm not sure now what I was basing that on.

I met him at the zoo. He was with his twin nephews, who were about six and giving him a very hard time. I was on my own. I've always counted the zoo as one of my private guilty pleasures. If you go alone you can choose exactly what to see (penguins, lions, bears) and what order to see it in, (bears, lions, penguins) and you can eat ice cream and stop for coffee whenever you're ready and not be dragged off to see monkeys and insects, both of which I feel are overrated.

I heard the nephews from about half a mile away. Poor Greg was doing his best with them, but they had discovered that the most fun you could have in a zoo full of exotic and wonderful species from all over the world was to pull your brother's hair, kick your uncle's legs and scream that you were hungry, tired, bored or in need of a wee, All the time.

Then one of the boys broke free and ran away, cannoning into me, and screaming that his uncle was trying to feed him to alligators.

At least when I'd smiled sympathetically, and then approached cautiously, and been introduced to the demon uncle and the other small man, there were two of us to two of them, and after a decent interval and some tea on the ambitiously named Bamboo Terrace, we were in a position where we could control one child each. I took mine to see bears and after quite a bit of whining, he settled down and agreed in a five-year-old way, that he was enjoying himself. I've always liked bears best, so we had that in common. When we were reunited with Greg and number two, he didn't seem to have considered the possibility that I might be a sad childless psychopath with intent to steal a five-year old, dye his hair and call him my own. Or if he had considered the possibility, he had obviously decided it to be the lesser of two evils. Or perhaps he thought that the one he'd be left with was the lesser of the two evils. We called them the Tweevils ever after that.

When I agreed to go for a drink with him later in the week, he took me to Claridges and gave me champagne. Call me shallow, but that sort of sealed it.

Anyway, we had been going out together for a while, and everything seemed nice and normal and I left Art College with a half-hearted diploma which was the product of last minute hard work rather than talent. I got the job as a stylist on a pretty interiors magazine, so we had even more money, and we lived in a flat in Chiswick, on the river, which I loved, and we had loads of friends, and Jenna lived within walking distance, and we went on holidays to Spain and Tuscany and listened to cool Eighties music, until one day, Greg said he thought we should get married. In fact he waited until Valentine's Day to ask me, which Jenna cited as the Number One reason why I should say No, on the grounds that it showed him to be completely without imagination.

Jenna was agonizing over Rod at the time. I remember thinking how terribly tiring it was, all that weeping and wailing and gnashing of teeth, all that travelling round after him, arriving in Manchester, or Birmingham, or Hull, to find him holed up in some dreary dive, as often as not with some teenage groupie. How I begged her to call it a day, to find someone who was worthy of her, who was reliable, dependable, safe. 'I'd die without him' she said, forgetting that what with the road crashes in his dodgy tour bus, and the drinking and the persistent bouts of depression, she was more likely to die with him. Poor Jenna, I thought, she needs to find someone like Greg. I said that to her once, but she laughed hysterically and threatened to throw herself under a bus.

One of the secrets of great cooking I believe, is when you can savour not only the great taste of the finished dish, but when you can still identify and enjoy all the individual ingredients within it. I wish that I had known that, on my wedding day, when the finished recipe was me, and I sailed up the aisle of St Stephen in the Marsh, in floor length cream silk, looking for all the world like a sofa on castors, and the individual ingredients were relief, vague concern that I couldn't recognize anyone in the pews, and persistent, nagging doubt.

I remember thinking, as I passed the font, my father holding my right arm in a vice-like grip, presumably counting the cost of the reception and determining that nothing should deter him from getting his money's worth, that I had never owned my own apartment. That I had never learned to sing. That at twenty two, this 'till death do us part' could actually be for more than sixty years. That it was three times my known lifetime, and yet I was promising to do something really quite difficult for all of it. I remember thinking that I would never ride a horse in Arizona, or sail a yacht in the Aegean. That I had never been to Borneo.

But you couldn't say that my marriage to Greg was a failure. I mean it lasted twenty years. It produced Hugo. It was all fine. Until Lucie.

What was he thinking? That an attractive, nineteen-year old girl in a denim shirt would really find a forty-seven-year-old Chartered Surveyor irresistible? That he was the answer to her dreams? If he had been David Cassidy, or David Essex maybe (although neither of them looks quite how I remember them these days). Or if he was a millionaire (make that billionaire for inflation, you can't buy a decent nine-bedroom mansion with gym and indoor pool complex in Surrey for less than five mill these days). Or if he was a rock musician, or an artist, and she could fall under the spell of his phenomenal talent. But my poor Greg is none of these things. He's just Greg, husband to me, father to Hugo, everyday man.

He was presumably thinking that I wouldn't find out, which was optimistic to say the least. After all I had nothing much to do but notice things. Either that, or he thought that if I did find out, I wouldn't mind.

The thing is, that all men tell fibs. All of them. Now mostly, they tell little ones, about things that don't matter. 'I came straight home, I only had one, I didn't get your message, I did stop at the shop but they didn't have any'.

My Mother once told me that the secret is, to let them get away with it. Because if you don't, if you accuse, or even prove, that he is lying, you are inadvertently teaching him how to get better at it. And then, just when you think you can spot a lie at a hundred yards, he tells a really big one. And you don't see it, because he is now a real Expert. He has graduated with a 2:1 Degree from the School of Lying to You.

I knew from the start about Lucie. I know, I said earlier that I had no idea, and indeed my conscious self hadn't registered even the possibility, but looking back on it, I knew. Her sucking up to me, her frequent visits to see Hugo when he clearly had no interest in pursuing the relationship (perhaps he also sensed that she was after, shall we say, the more mature man). The strange and enormously wide variety of outfits we saw over the few months we welcomed her into our home.

And then there was Greg's Mentionitis. It's a dreadful disease when it strikes the illicit lover. "Have you seen Lucie lately? How is Lucie? I was thinking Hugo, that Lucie might be interested in... Now she reminds me of your friend Lucie..." Yes, Mentionitis is better at proclaiming you have a more than usual interest in another person than a persistent sneeze, runny eyes and an itchy nose are for proclaiming that you have hay fever.

In *By the Time I get to Phoenix* mode, The Ballad of Lucie and Greg ran for at least six verses before the Big Discovery. By the time you get home, she will be sitting at the table doing her homework with your son, By the time you ring your husband at the hotel she will have checked out of his room. By the time you discover that partners were, in fact, invited to the summer drinks, his colleagues will have been briefed to say she was on work experience. By the time the Credit Card bill comes he will have made up a story about sending flowers to his mother. By the time you identify the scent on his jacket as being definitely Not Yours, he will have invented a damsel in distress on the train, and By the time you find a black lace bra (34B and definitely not a possibility for a size 36D fortyish woman) tangled in his shirt in the laundry basket, he will have run out of excuses and accuse Hugo of being careless with his girlfriends.

By the time Hugo finds a rather roundabout way to tell you he has never had a girlfriend at all, never mind one who sheds La Perla around other people's bedrooms, the game will have long been Up. Icarus really was a dream.

I never really had it out with Greg. I mean when things came to a head, and I came home early and found them in the bath together. I just looked and looked, and what I remember most clearly is the level of that valuable and expensive bath oil in its lovely glass bottle.

People talk about worlds coming crashing down on them, about single moments destroying everything in their path, and I suppose it was a bit like that. I felt shocked, I felt like an intruder in my own home. I felt old, and fat, and ugly and unwanted. I felt stupid because deep down I don't think I was entirely surprised. But mostly, as I stared at two naked people, one decidedly more familiar than the other but both shiny with bathwater and energy, I felt overdressed. I think I may even have taken my cardigan off.

I thought afterwards that if Greg had been able to come up with almost any excuse to explain I might have forgiven him, on the grounds of marvellous inventiveness beyond the call of duty, but he didn't. He sort of sat there, the bubbles making an additional white roll of fat round his middle, his fingers like uncooked dough, whilst Lucie leapt out of the bath and wrapped one of my better towels round her staggeringly lovely body and said, "It's not what you think."

The scent of Jo Malone Nutmeg and Ginger will never be the same to me now. But I had pretty well moved on to Amber and Lavender, by then so in the end it wasn't a terrible loss. I went straight out and bought more, just a day later. A whole twenty four hours after my twenty-year marriage was officially ended and there I was, shopping happily, treating myself to bath products. Watch and Learn, Woman Left by a Man heading for Phoenix.

I didn't see Lucie again, in the flesh as it were. I saw her in my head. I don't know if Greg saw her again. He said not, but then he also said it had meant nothing. As if that would help - that he wrecked my life and our marriage for nothing.

"It was wrong," he said, "But it took this for me to realize now, how good our marriage is."

"Was," I corrected him. "And it's funny you should say that, because I've just realized how very bad it was."

We limped on for a bit, mainly because I couldn't decide what kind of crutches we needed to achieve decent movement. That was how I managed to get to the airport on that fateful morning, in my wraparound dress, just doing my duty as a wife, being me, reliable, dependable, Joanne the woman for whom having sex with someone you aren't married to is, at the very least, out of character.

I wondered if the problem was in me. Is everything not good enough, at the time you have it? Is more of the same, the best you should hope for?

"Divorce is hell," Jenna said, when I asked her why she never married Rod, even when Seven was born. I thought it was so sad, that she thought of divorce as an inevitable consequence of marriage. Her parents had got a divorce when she was about eleven, and she had been caught up in what the neighbours had called a 'tug of love'. Better than a tug of indifference we thought, especially as it resulted in a Sony Walkman and several new pairs of jeans for Jenna.

My divorce won't be hell, mainly because I won't be there when it happens. If it happens. I have no plans, and not divorcing must be the best possible precaution against getting married again. Even if I really really want to, in a moment of weakness, I won't be able to, and my beloved will have to kneel and propose in vain, and pine away for the love of me and writhe in insecurity that I might one day leave him and go to Borneo. Or Phoenix.

Chapter Fifteen : New-Found Land

Most of the people on this plane are now standing up, clambering about, walking unsteadily like small children, clutching at seat backs and landing awkwardly on each other. We are all pretty desperate to walk about now, to prove we still have feeling in our legs, that our feet still work. The air crew have all but disappeared, and are no doubt mustering their strength for the last trundle through the aisle with the soggy boxed breakfasts which are supposedly an incentive for us to sit down and behave until the plane lands.

I, too, feel the urge to walk. I have been pretty good so far, remarkably unfidgety. Malcolm is still asleep beside me, and I reckon I can just about climb over him without waking him up, if I can just get my leg....ah, oof.

"Well hello again," says Malcolm, "are you reconsidering your decision about the Mile High Club?"

I try and focus. My eyes are about six inches from his. I am sort of astride him, with one leg on either side of his pull-down tray, which juts out between my thighs like a little runway all its own. I feel sure he is about to make a remark about taxiing or doors to manual. I have no idea what to do or say, and spend several seconds wishing I was dead. Malcolm extends the only limb which isn't pinned down by me, his left arm, and uses it to propel me back over him and down into my own seat. I pretend that I have already been for a little walk along the aisle and was trying to return, and give up all hope of ever walking again.

Along the length of the plane, people are edging along, covering the length of the plane at 0.001 kilometres an hour whilst the plane itself is still hurtling through the air in the other direction at about 900 kilometres miles per hour. At this proximity people-watching is barely satisfactory, because there is almost no room for speculation at all. Everything is up close and obvious.

Like the married couple who haven't said a word to each other since we boarded, but whenever either of them gets up, the other whips out a forbidden mobile phone and texts madly to a lover.

And the red-haired man in dress-down Friday business clothes, who is conquering the market with a new range of packaging machines. He has several meetings in New York and will then travel onto Las Vegas where there is a huge global packaging machinery conference. Thanks to his conversations with anyone near enough to listen and his constant dictation into a little machine, I know so much about his machinery and am so familiar with his itinerary that I could attend in his place if he has an unfortunate accident on the way through the terminal building when we land. I could launch an entire career in packaging machinery.

There is the couple from Row Forty who go up and down the aisle together, whispering, clearly not realizing that whispers carry far further than low voices. I have become rather fond of these two, they are young and in love and they are going to meet a surrogate mother who has agreed to have their baby. I hope the surrogate mother is nice and wonder vaguely how the visa and passport thing will work out. I wonder how two people from England can enter the US and three come back.

I wanted to have at least five children, especially after I had Hugo. I saw myself at the head of a big noisy family, rustling up magnificent food at all hours in a kitchen surrounded by young people, who would sit round the table and talk about the world with new, young vision. Well there was a kitchen table, but what that young person was doing on it with my husband was frankly not what I had in mind.

No more children came, and I went to doctors who said they couldn't see a problem, but Greg didn't like the idea of 'other people mucking about with us', and that was in the days just before you were allowed to make that decision on your own, rather than with your 'partner' and anyway we had Hugo, so I was jolly lucky. I only mind occasionally.

Now there's the smuggler. He has been up and down hundreds of times, he looks more uncomfortable than a fat bridesmaid in a Pronuptia showroom. Whatever is he smuggling, in his anonymous looking luggage so many feet below us in the hold? However did he get into the smuggling game? It's not as if he's any good at it. Look at him, stands out a mile. I'd stop him straightaway, if I was a Customs official. But then maybe it's a double bluff. It couldn't possibly be him, because he stands out a mile. Being a Customs Official probably isn't as easy as it seems.

The giggling and shrieking is coming from the back of the plane, where half a dozen teenagers are on a school trip. Their teachers are exhausted already and, being teachers of some twenty years' experience each, are now immune to enthusiasm. They don't see why it's necessary for children to go on these extravagant trips. In their day it was a day out at the Tower of London and pray nobody was sick on the coach on the way home. By the time 5C have taken in the Empire State Building, the

Guggenheim, the Museum of Modern Art and the Met, at least one of them will have been arrested for jaywalking, two will have lost a valuable electronic item which will have to be reported, claimed on insurance and replaced, one of them will have gone AWOL for twenty four hours and one will be pregnant.

The queue makes its way up and down the plane, people squeezing their way through, as if there was somewhere to go, flexing wrists and ankles like newly hatched long-legged birds, following the instructions in the How not to get Deep Vein Thrombosis leaflet in the seat pocket. I can't move at all for fear of exciting Malcolm further, so presumably I will drop dead with a blockage in my aortic artery within hours of beginning my new life in America.

I can at least flick through magazines, and pulling a rather dog-eared copy of Vogue out of the pocket I spend an hour or so looking at clothes, and shoes and handbags, advertisements for cosmetics, and articles about fashion designers and actresses and European Royals. Up here, in the middle of nowhere, it all seems completely unreal, as if it's all just been made up by a creative director, a fantasy land where the blemish-free people all look lovely and the sun always shines, and nobody needs an umbrella, or has to stand in a bus queue, and men know exactly what to wear, a world which smells beautiful, thanks to the free sachet of Tom Ford Portofino Neroli attached to page 54, and where nobody needs to eat, and everyone goes to fabulous functions and drinks champagne in rooms full of high art and the aforementioned European princesses.

Looking out of the window, I can see that we have descended slightly, to just below cloud level and way, way down underneath us, is land.

Consulting the map on the screen in front of me, I see that this is Newfoundland.

I've always been curious about inhospitable lands. As a child I was fascinated by Baffin island, and later, you will remember, got a bit hung up on the idea of Borneo. Newfoundland is one of those places which just looks so impossible, all wild storms and freezing barren landscapes, and (not surprisingly) angry people. It was originally colonized by Indians, and Vikings, and then by the Brits, in the 1600s, who colonized it for three hundred or so years before signing it over to Canada. It has given its name to a dog, a sheep and a pony. Looking through the 'Information About Your Journey' section of the in-flight magazine, I see that Newfoundland is also the sea-bird capital of North America.   Looking down from here, through the tiny little window in this stuffy hot cabin, it looks like miles and miles of rock and snow, with a few tiny isolated buildings. For most of the year the average temperature in Newfoundland is freezing point, although in the summer it can rocket up to, oh all of 25 degrees. And I can almost see Judi Dench and Kevin Spacey, figuring it all out together, battling the terrors of the elements in the film. I'm probably the only person on this flight who secretly wishes the plane had to divert and land at the nearest airport, and that it should be a desolate snowbound landing strip, right down there in the middle of nowhere. Then I could get out, and look around and I would know what Somewhere Else was like.

Chapter Sixteen : Which Leads me to Colin

I think I mentioned Colin Pitt earlier. But not in a mentionitis sort of way, so you may have forgotten about him. The thing is he's at least part of the reason for all this.

Colin was a business contact my husband made, whilst on a conference in Warrington. The conference was on the ecological significance of glass in urban development. Greg had been away for the whole week, so I assumed it had been a very important conference, lots of things to talk about, some Very Big Decisions to be made. Later I found out that it had been a two-day meeting in a Best Western, and Greg had spent the rest of the week in a very expensive hotel in the Lake District. According to the letter of welcome I found in the glovebox of the car, tucked inside our copy of '100 Great British Walks', he was there with me, Mrs Greg West, but I feel sure I would have remembered. Walking isn't my favourite thing (which is probably why he felt safe using the treacherous letter as a bookmark for that particular volume) but indoor thermal spas and luxurious four poster beds are right up my street. However, I was nowhere near that street of course, so I can only suppose that the 'interim' Mrs West had a lovely time instead of me.

But I can't complain. If Greg had never gone to Warrington, he would never have been given the contact details of one of the world's greatest experts in the use of glass in city centres. And he would never have emailed him to discuss the new BT building planned for the centre of Reading, and then the world's greatest expert would never have factored the UK into his European round of speaking engagements and I would never have gone to the airport to meet him.

I don't know what I was expecting as I stood there in the Arrivals hall, with too much sugar and coffee in my system and not enough make-up on. I think I was probably looking for someone who looked like Greg, only American, whatever I might have meant by that. Probably a man with the same graying, thinning hair, lined graying face, a slightly flabby waistline and the distinct look of the beaten dog about him, but possibly wearing a pale blue button-down shirt and pleat-front chinos with deck shoes, because that's what all the American businessmen I had ever seen wore.

So I wasn't looking for Colin at all. Nevertheless he found me, possibly because of the 'Colin Pitt' sign I had in my hand, but even as I looked straight at him, and he at me, I still didn't make the connection.

The man who stopped in front of me was about three inches taller than Greg, so about six foot one. He had thick wavy dark hair, with just a hint of grey at the temples, and grey eyes, the colour of the most expensive kind of cat, those long haired blue-ish jobs with the sad faces and the attitude. He was wearing the loveliest suit I had ever seen on a man, a very soft charcoal material with almost no detailing on it all, and it was a perfect fit. His shoes, which I was by then looking at in some awe and wonder, were polished English brogues. Behind him was a beautiful, battered brown leather holdall, with proper handles, and definitely no wheels.

I'm thinking Cary Grant. With a bit of Gabriel Byrne. I'm thinking who is this, and where is Colin Pitt. And I'm thinking that Colin Pitt may have to find his own way to Henley because I'm not dropping everything to go searching round this airport for him. I have a life. And this is it.

"Hi," said Cary Grant.

"Hello you," I said.

"Are you looking for me?" he said.

Well there were a number of possible answers to that question. 'Absolutely', was one of them. Or, 'I have been looking for you for my whole life. You are in my dreams, you are in my heart, I feel as though I have known you for ever'. There are more answers, all along the same lines.

"Technically, I'm waiting for someone else," I said.

"Technically?" The substantial eyebrows were raised slightly, in an interested and probably slightly amused way. Whatever way it was, it had the effect of dissolving my heart, which sort of whooshed in my chest and caused me to turn into a performing seal. I mean I was virtually clapping my hands.

"Well. I mean I was supposed to. Meet someone. I mean, if he's here, well fine, but if he isn't well, it just doesn't really matter does it?" I said. "I mean here. Nothing really matters does it? Everyone will presumably get to wherever they want to go won't they? In the end. That's the point of an airport isn't it?" (Ark Ark, throw another brightly coloured ball for me to balance).

"He might have missed you in this crowd," Cary Grant pointed out.

"Well, he's a grown man. I mean, I expect he is. He can sort himself out I daresay. He's probably made other arrangements already. Americans are very efficient that way I've found."

"A stranger in a strange country?" Cary Grant was obviously trying not to laugh at me. "He might be confused, lost even. He might be rather upset to see how quickly you are prepared to forget about him."

"Oh I doubt it. He's an expert on something or other. I should think he's very used to airports."

"He's probably used to being met, if he's that important."

"Well, perhaps someone else met him. Anyway, I don't need to, well, I suppose I should..."

"Was he on the same plane as I was? Virgin566 from San Francisco?"

I had forgotten. "I think so," I said.

"Well I might recognize him. Perhaps we should look for him together."

Cary Grant began to look round at the lessening tide of incoming passengers, grey faced and world-weary, the last of them being the great Un-met, the ones in no particular hurry with nothing important to do and no real excitement at being in England at all. Cary Grant and I watched them together until the rear was soundly brought up by the cabin crew, spruced up, high with relief at having dumped another four hundred or so people in a new country and ready to go straight out and flirt with other.

"How do they walk in those?" I said vaguely, as three identical women in vertiginous red shoes strode by, sex on legs in triplicate. "You'd think their feet would swell up on the plane. Mine do."

Great. Now I'd drawn attention to unbeatable competition and given him a vision of fluid-retaining ankles. Just the balancing ball to drop and the performance would be complete.

"So what do you think? Shall we try and find him? The person you've come to meet?" he suggested.

"Together?" I said. To be honest I was rather surprised he was still standing next to me and not halfway across the concourse striding arm in arm with Richard Branson's Beverley Sisters. "Well that would be... I mean, you probably have to go somewhere, or.."

"Do you have his name?"

"His name? Oh, well, you know how it is, I can't seem to remember. Silly isn't it, how these things just go right out of your head.." (Marvellous. Now I have Alzheimers').

Cary Grant reached out a hand and gently took the sign from me. Holding it at arms' length as if it was difficult to read, and not in fact clearly written in red felt pen letters six inches high, he said "Colin Pitt."

"Oh. Right." I said unenthusiastically, failing to notice that he had pronounced it Coh-Linn. Pitt as in Brad. "That'll be him."

"Actually, that'll be me," he said.

"Oh no," I said, "It can't possibly be you."

"Interesting," he said, "Why not?"

"Well because Colin Pitt is a much older man," I said. "I'm sure he is. He's a professor of something." And in my head I added, 'because Colin Pitt is part of my husband's life, and you belong to me'.

"OK," said Cary Grant. "I tell you what, why don't you and I go to the cocktail bar and consider the options?"

"There isn't a cocktail bar," I said sadly, "there's a Smart Subs and a Starbucks and a WH Smith and some kind of pub. This is England."

"There is a cocktail bar in the Virgin Atlantic Upper Class Lounge," he said. And there was. In a few short minutes there was also a performing seal in a faded wraparound dress and a saggy cardigan without enough make-up on. Mind you, there was enough make up in the Upper Class Lounge to cover the entire female population of South East England, and that was just on the two members of staff. And one of them was a man.

"Now," said Cary Grant, handing me a glass of champagne. "What shall we do about Colin Pitt?"

I told you I was shallow.

"A bugger about Colin's plane being so delayed," Greg said much later, when I finally got home. "Who would have thought it? Nine hours, that's a really bad one. I can't imagine how the poor chap felt, after being up there for so long. I bet he was glad to get to his hotel. Poor you love, you must have been hanging about there for ever!"

"For ever. I wish," I said.

But Greg had already turned the television on.

Chapter Seventeen : Of Love and En-Suite Bathrooms

When you are in love it seems as though you have never been there before. That's how we're programmed, so we don't die when one love ends. We think we'll die, and indeed, we want to, but in the end, we don't. And when we fall in love again, despite ourselves, we realise that what we had before, the thing we lost, the thing which nearly killed us, wasn't love at all. We know that, now we have a chance to compare it with this.

All I knew is that before I men Colin, whenever I thought of love, I thought of it as something for other people. Then, all the week following my meeting with Colin, I thought of him, and I thought of me. We were just meant to be together. I stopped worrying about what I looked like. Hell, I forgot what I looked like altogether. I didn't care, it didn't matter. And as a result, I looked better than I had for years. I lost weight, my hair and skin glowed. My teeth shone, probably as a result of being exposed to so much more light, with all the smiling. I found that pink suited me, when I had always believed it made me look like ham. I suddenly had an urge to have a good clear out at home, and went through the house like a whirlwind, turning out cupboards and filling bin bags and boxes by the dozen, carting them off to the tip or the charity shop, and only occasionally having to return and buy something back when I realised I had gone too far. I wore beads and scarves and hats, discovered during my comprehensive clear outs of long-neglected drawers. It was as though I was a mole, emerging from a long, long hibernation into the sun, blinking and surprised.

Greg came back one evening and said he was glad I was at home because if I had been out, he would have assumed we'd moved. I barely heard him, because I was reading texts. Streams of them. Colin was good at texting.

The words of songs become important when you are in love. Everything has meaning. The birds sing for you, the sun comes out for you, the rain is beautiful, it makes the pavements shine for you. When you are together the world stops turning, and when you leave one another's company, you can hardly believe that so much time has passed. It's like going to the cinema in the afternoon, you are lost and nobody can find you, and it's just delicious.

The decision to go to bed with Colin Pitt, when it came to it, wasn't a big decision at all. It wasn't like stepping off a cliff, or throwing caution to the wind, it was far simpler than that. I can't even remember the in-between bit, the bit after the porter has shown you all the things in the room while you scream inside for him to go away because you don't care about the tea and coffee things, you won't be watching television, you already know how to turn lights on and off and nobody ever uses the trouser press. the bit before you find yourself in a huge bed you haven't had to make, with no clothes on, with a man you don't know and a bottle of champagne cooling in a bucket beside you.

I supposed it helped that I wasn't the first adulterer in my marriage. But actually, I'm not convinced it would have made a difference either way.

Things I didn't think about: being flabby round the middle, the fact that my highlights could do with renewing, the supermarket, the mince I should have taken out of the freezer in time for supper, the money it would cost to get my car out of the car park, Greg.

Things I did think about: Vivaldi, caramel waffles, roses in gardens, and roses in vases. Rain on umbrellas, spreading oak trees, white yachts in blue seas. Being happy.

Jenna knew immediately of course. "What the hell has happened to you?" she said, two days after I had spent nearly eight hours in a suite in the Radisson Edwardian Heathrow with a man whose plane hadn't been late at all.

I was a bit embarrassed. A grown woman having to own up to having had sex with someone who wasn't her husband, and liking it so much she could think of nothing else. A woman who had been married for years, with a grown up son, believing herself in love for the first time. Ridiculous.

"Told you so," said Jenna.

On the Tuesday, Greg met Colin himself, when they both went to the Seminar on Bonding Glass with Steel at the Innovation Centre in Milton Keynes. I was a bit on edge all day, in case Colin let something slip, but when he got back all Greg said was, "Pitt knows his stuff, I can tell you. We could do with him on our team full-time. I wonder if he would be interested in a sabbatical in the UK?" Then I found I was disappointed that Colin hadn't let anything slip. How could he avoid talking about it, about me? I could barely speak for suppressing the desire to shout from the rooftops, 'I'm in love!' and 'I'm happy!' and 'Colin Pitt loves me!' I felt as though I had a sign on my head, a big neon sign which read 'This Woman is Having a Love Affair!'

On Wednesday afternoon, in the sumptuous bathroom of Room 104 at the Malmaison in Oxford, I put Greg's suggestion about the sabbatical to Colin and he laughed, sending bubbles round the room. "Now there's an idea," he said, but not seriously.

"But it would be lovely if I could see you again. That is, all the time," I said wistfully, quite a lot later. Already I was struggling with the knowledge that Colin's flight back to the US was only a couple of days away. I knew I was beginning to sound desperate. Jenna would have been so cross with me.

He said he loved my hair, and he said he loved the way I spoke, and the funny way I walked, and he said he loved talking to me, and being with me, so that was pretty much the same as saying he loved me, wasn't it. How can you love someone's hair, and not love them?

On Thursday afternoon I told Greg I was having dinner with Jenna and would probably spend the night at hers. He was thrilled because the Pig and Fiddle in Henley was showing the Big Match, Live. Luckily I remembered at the last minute to text Jenna, because halfway through the evening Greg phoned Jenna to ask me if it was OK to cook frozen prawns straight from the freezer. Jenna told him that I'd said yes, but obviously I'd found out that he hadn't died of food poisoning by the time she told me the story.

Colin and I went to Le Manoir de Quat Saisons. I know. It was quite the most marvellous thing I have ever done, and that might include having Hugo. It was an unseasonably warm evening, and the moonlight lit up the gardens as we had a post-dinner walk before retiring to the prettiest room in the world. For goodness' sake, is a girl really supposed to resist?

In the morning, I was only vaguely aware of Colin leaving, the hotel was so discreet with the wakeup call, and he was spirited away by taxi to the airport, leaving me behind in a cloud of soft lemony manliness, and I was weeping so much that I almost missed the little present he had left on the bedside table. Inside a pale blue bag was a pale blue box tied with a white ribbon. Oh yes. Tiffany.

I savoured the moments before opening it. I'm a girl who likes to fully appreciate every moment of life's good bits. I thought about the champagne, and the souffle, and the roasted duck and the deconstructed apple charlotte, the Condrieu, (which I discovered was my favourite wine ever, despite never having tasted it before), and the fabulous, rich coffee, and I remembered going back to the room and Colin making love to me with the curtains open so the moonlight fell across the pillow, and I remembered the last things we said, as we drifted off to sleep.

"You know you should come see me," he said. Americans eh? They leave out the unnecessary words, like 'and'. Funny how before Colin, that used to drive me insane.

"In New York?" I said.

"Well, that's where I live!"

"Just me?"

"Unless Greg wants to join us. We could talk about filtration systems for recyclable glass."

How could I possibly manage to get myself to America without Greg? I thought, although I was already imagining myself at the airport. How would I go to America to see my lover without my husband finding out?

"I could invent a relative," I suggested.

"Sure you could Jo-Jo, you could invent a relative who lives in America that you've never mentioned in eighteen years of marriage. I don't think Greg is a dumb-ass." Colin said.

"I could pretend I got a job," I tried.

"Without an interview? And without a salary? No good either."

"Or I could pretend I was going somewhere else. On a course to learn something. Watercolours in Eastbourne. Pottery in the Lake District. Better? But not without flaws, actually. I'd have to buy bad watercolours or wonky pots on the way home. But perhaps...?"

"You could tell him you're with your friend, what's her name?"

Of course. How did he think of that before I did?

"Jenna. Of course. Although then she would have to screen all her calls while I was away, so she didn't pick up if it was him."

"But it wouldn't be him. He'll think she's on holiday. With you."

Colin was good at this.

"And if I did come. To America. To see you?"

Colin lay back on the pillows, the blue moon making the very best of his profile, the slight sheen on his very good skin, his hair still damp from all the exercise. He appeared deep in thought as he laid out an itinerary for the trip I knew I'd never be able to make.

"We would start with the Bubble Lounge, on Canal Street. And then the Four Seasons. As a sort of homage to this place. Quat Saisons. We could find Four Seasonses all over the world. And we could drive up the coast to Martha's Vineyard, hang out with the surfers. I've got a small place up there I use for summer breaks. We could go fishing. You should come. I'd love to show you my city."

"I've shown you mine, now you show me yours?"

"Exactly."

"Although I showed you Reading."

"And Oxford."

"You'd already seen Oxford!"

"But not with you. And Reading was a bonus."

It was difficult to tell if he was teasing me. "Liar," I said, deciding.

"Come and see me, you lovely girl?" he said, more seriously, looking right at me.

"Well maybe I will. Maybe I will....I will. I do." Even afterwards, as I lay there in the dark I couldn't decide if I had said the last bit out loud or not.

Inside the pale blue Tiffany box was a dark blue velvet box and inside the dark blue velvet box was a small, white-gold champagne flute, edged with tiny white diamonds, on a long chain.

Wow.

Chapter Eighteen : Maple Syrup and Limoncello

Jenna says there's wisdom in the air everywhere, but we only hear it when we listen. Personally whenever I find myself on the horns of a dilemma I find it difficult to hear anything, except the trivial background noise of my life. Lost trainers, shopping lists, missed trains, malfunctioning software, television game shows, I think over the years I have given up trying to think about important things   at all, and as a result have forgotten how to do it.

And if ever I needed wisdom, that was the time. I wandered the Earth feeling the little gold champagne glass against my skin inside my sweaters, my phone in one hand, longing for a text, hating every message which wasn't from him. I felt as though with every step, every hour and every day I was becoming less and less of myself, as if by waiting, I was using myself up, and with nothing to replace me, I would empty out altogether.

For the first week after Colin had gone back to New York, I just drifted through the days, flopping in and out of rooms, floating up and down supermarket aisles, gazing out of windows. Whenever a plane went over I would look up at it for as long as possible, tracing its progress across the sky and imagining it was on its way to America, carrying hundreds of lucky people who within hours would be within touching distance of him.

Every plane was a possible source of rescue for me, even the ones which were almost certainly charter flights filled to bursting with pale and desperate holidaymakers on their way to Malaga.

Hugo did notice something had changed in me, but only after I mixed his white sports socks with a coloured wash and forgot to get any milk in despite having appeared to spend all day in Sainsburys. I think that was the day I decided to look for American products, to see if they were different from English ones. As a result I had filled the fridge with Maple Syrup and the bread bin with American-style pancakes, and the cupboards with Granola (which is pretty much a mixture of Muesli and Grape Nuts as far as I can gather, and is still there, in the cupboard above the worktop, on the left of the cooker, because it's inedible).

"What's the matter with you these days Mum?" he said vaguely, coming into the kitchen holding a purplish-pink sock in each hand and rifling through the fridge looking for something to eat which didn't call for cooking, cutlery, or sitting down. "There isn't any bread. And we're out of orange juice again. You used to be good at this stuff!"

Used to be. I used to be good at shopping and laundry. I used to be good. I used to be.

At the weekend, Greg had been asked to go to a conference in Brighton, to deliver a paper on the work he and Colin had been doing. He asked me if I wanted to go with him, which was odd, because he'd never done that before. Presumably Lucie was busy. He thought I didn't know he was still seeing her, but I knew alright. I just didn't care. It was no longer relevant, in the way that cooking, eating, cleaning the house, or filling in car insurance forms were no longer relevant. I suppose it was out of a combination of guilt and curiosity. I said I would go to Brighton.

We spent a night in this desperate little hotel on the seafront, all Georgian bay windows and howling draughts. The 'new management' had re-styled the interior as a 'boutique' which meant there was a huge freestanding bathtub in the bedroom and the loo was a 'wetroom' with a shower head in the ceiling, so you had to move all the loo paper and all the cleaning products and towels out before you could have a shower, and remember to put the loo paper back again before you used the loo. There was nowhere to hang anything, not even ourselves, which was probably a good thing because by Sunday morning that was about the only thing we felt like doing.

Greg had to go to the Conference dinner on the Saturday evening, so I took myself out to an Italian place behind the Brighton Pavilion. Colin had mentioned the Pavilion, but he'd never seen it, so I planned to take a picture on my phone for him, but when I got there it was floodlit in pink and purple and it looked like an outsized Indian restaurant. I thought it was probably better left to the imagination.

The Italians were very attentive. Thank heavens they know how to treat a lone female diner. Most restaurants seat you by the kitchen, sweep the other place setting away with a disappointed flourish and ignore you for the rest of the evening, unless you ask to see the dessert menu, in which case they raise an eyebrow as if to say 'and you wonder why you are eating alone?' And when they do, I want to order the sticky toffee pudding as an act of defiance, but instead give in, and find myself saying 'just coffee thanks'.

Colin had always insisted we had pudding. "It's the true test of a restaurant," he said, "So many great restaurants don't bother with it. Besides, I want to savour every minute of everything I do with you, so the longer we can make it last, the better." That was kind of a thing with him, making it last, if you get my meaning.

However, even the attentive Italians' interest began to wane when I was the only diner left, turning the background music up and up, so even I had to bow to the great God, Julio Iglesias, and leave. As had all the girls he'd loved before presumably. I'd had a very large brandy as well as that sticky lemon liqueur stuff they give you in Italian restaurants to make you think they love you, so I thought it was funny and walked back to the hotel along the seafront laughing and looking at the moon on the shingle and wishing for Colin.

When I got back Greg had dumped his dinner jacket in the bathtub and gone to sleep, lying diagonally across the mean little double bed. The moonlight lit up the back of his head, reflecting on his bald patch.

Later at home, as I emptied the overnight bags into the washing machine, wondering how it is that there's always far more in a suitcase when you bring it home than there was when you packed it to go away, and how horrible and tired it all looks, I found the hotel receipt for our stay in an inside pocket of Greg's 'Sunday' jacket, a tweed-ish thing usually worn with corduroys and with a distinct air of geography teacher about it. In the envelope with the bill in it was another one of those letters that hotels leave in the rooms to make you think they're thrilled to have you. 'Welcome Back Mr and Mrs West' it said.

I couldn't decide what I was more unhappy about, the fact that Greg had been to the Seacrest Hotel before, with someone else, or that having been there once, he'd seriously thought it was nice enough to go again.

Chapter Nineteen : Mathematics

Funnily enough, Jenna was right about the wisdom. And when I eventually heard it, it was when I least expected to. On the Monday after Brighton, I decided to treat myself to lunch in Oxford with Jenna. She said she had something Important to tell me, so we booked a table on the top floor of the Ashmolean for lunch. I was much too early as usual, so I headed for my favourite coffee place, just opposite the entrance to Lincoln College. I love Lincoln. As you peer in through the outer doors, past the Porter's lodge, its all ivy and creeper, and appropriately green. I like to imagine I am a don, scurrying about between the vines and the staircases, books under my arm, my head full of knowledge and the air round me full of the curious interest of the less clever. I am a leading expert on something, my published papers are eagerly awaited, people write to me from all over the world, especially America, especially New York, especially Colin. Except he hadn't written, so I came back to Earth outside The Missing Bean with a bump.

The Bean is always packed with student-types so you can be sure of some good eavesdropping, although iphones and keyboards have put paid to a lot of the traditional conversation. Sometimes I could swear that two people sitting across a two-foot wide table are communicating with each other via email.

I was thinking about Colin and America. I was slightly low on reasonable excuses for him. I'd only sent three messages (at least three too many, said Jenna when I told her), but I was aching to send another, like a reforming smoker aches for a cigarette.

There are plenty of really bad excuses for not sending a text or email to the woman you love: Your phone ran out of battery (no it didn't). You were in a no-reception zone. (For days? Why? Are you a coalminer?) You were in a meeting. (What, you didn't break off in five hours even to go to the bathroom?). You did send texts and emails and you just can't imagine why she didn't get them (No you didn't).

And there are perfectly good excuses for not sending a text or email to the woman you love: You died.

But somehow I just knew Colin hadn't died. So the trouble was, I was running out of ways to re-configure the bad reasons and make them perfectly good ones.

There was a boy sitting at the next table, deep in a textbook. He had little headphones in his ears, and I wondered what Darwin would have made of this generation who have evolved to concentrate on reading one thing, while listening to something quite different and playing Call of Duty with someone in New Zealand. He looked a bit like Hugo, long legs slightly cramped up under the table, big feet threatening to trip others up. He was wearing one of those big hooded sweaters, over a pullover over a T-shirt, all hanging out over a low-slung jeans waistband. Surely if you're cold enough to need four layers, you'll feel the draught around your kidneys if you don't tuck any of them in?

The boy had fair hair too, like Hugo's, all messy and tangled, and my text-to-Colin-hungry fingers longed to run themselves through it. As I watched him happily working his multi-input brain, I was startled by the arrival of a second boy, equally over-sized, identically dressed and carrying a rucksack which threatened to sweep everyone aside. But even if I had been knocked to the floor by the rucksack I couldn't have been more surprised when Boy 2 kissed Boy 1 firmly on the lips and sat down. Their hands entwined, and then Boy 1 resumed his reading and Boy 2 got out a similar sort of book and they just looked so peaceful, like an old couple who had been married for forty years.

Then a beautiful woman in a raincoat came over to my table and did that silent asking thing with her eyebrows and her cappuccino, and I answered her with a nod and she sat in the seat opposite me.

"Thinking," she said to nobody in particular. "It's marvellous isn't it? How lucky we are to be able to think."

I must have been staring encouragingly at her, because she went on. "And everyone everywhere can do it, and do you know what, nothing and nobody can stop us!"

I found myself smiling at her, mainly because what I was actually thinking was how lovely the raincoat was and whether I could find one like it. The woman nodded at me and undid the belt. Underneath she had a sort of woollen dress in a lovely blackberry colour. Some people just get clothes right. I wondered if she was older or younger than me.

Then she rummaged in a bag and pulled out a book, which she put on the table. She put on some spectacles and then she tucked a pencil behind her ear and proceeded to read. Every now and then she took the pencil and made a note in the book.

In fact I had a book with me, but I didn't feel I could field a copy of *I Capture the Castle,* even if it was the thousandth time I'd read it and I always turned to it when lonely and confused, because the book she was reading was called *Cultural Sums: the Mathematical Properties of Twenty First Century Life*.

"It's not as bad as it sounds," she said suddenly, and I realised I had been staring again. "Actually it's quite fun."

I must have looked sceptical because she said "Basically it tells us that everything is maths. Time, birth and death, food and drink, painting, theatre, literature, there's a mathematical theory behind everything, if you choose to look for it."

"Art is mathematical?" I said. Perhaps that's why I got a Third in my Degree. I'd been working on a colour and shape principle, mixing paint, that kind of thing.

"Absolutely. I think so anyway. But it is rather my field. I'm a maths person. You look like a philosophy person."

Which was quite the nicest thing she could have said to a woman who had begun the dialogue by wondering how much another woman's coat had cost and whether she was older or younger.

"The great thing about knowing about the maths, is that you can use it to make decisions," she said, "Once you're aware of the mathematical principle, you can work with it until you find the right answer. Or at least an answer which works out."

And that was where I found the wisdom.

Chapter Twenty : Fig and Walnut Salad

Lunch started out by being lovely. We got a table right by the window and Jenna was only ten minutes late. I'm always at a table first, I'm always everywhere first. The trouble is, that leaves no incentive for anyone to be on time. By the time they arrive, I've already found a table, argued with someone to get a better one if necessary, repelled all possible sharers and probably opened the bar tab with my credit card. It's much nicer to arrive when someone else has already done all that. Still, at least it makes me feel useful. I do wonder if that's why people invite me.

Minutes I've spent on my own when other people have been late: 39,000.

I wanted to tell Jenna about raincoat woman but somehow I didn't get around to it. I did tell her about the Beautiful Boys though and that was a bit odd, because when I said how much Boy 1 reminded me of Hugo, she said, "no surprises there then" and gave me an odd, 'indulging your granny' kind of look.

As Jenna talked and the waiter brought two glasses of champagne, and a couple of huge menus, I found myself thinking in numbers. The number of times Greg and another Mrs West had stayed in hotels. (unknown = x) The number of successful washes I'd put through the faithful Indesit before I ran the coloureds into the whites (probably something in the region of 400) My age (45) the number of childhood ambitions I had fulfilled so far (1 if you count Hugo) the number of men I'd slept with (8 if you count Greg) the number of times I'd really loved sex (4 and that's all in one week and not counting Greg) the number of glasses of champagne I'd drunk to try and convince myself that my life was lovely (approximately 1000).

Jenna was onto a tale about Seven's father Rod, who still insisted on visiting every fortnight even though Seven wasn't at home.

"I just don't know what to do with him," she said, "I open the door and say Hello and he just sort of comes in and waits."

"What used to happen?" I said, "When Seven was a child?"

"I'd shout up the stairs and Seven would come down and they'd go out."

"Where did they go?"

"The cinema. His dreary flat over the laundrette in the High Street. Sometimes an exhibition. Parks. Lunch in McDonalds when she was small, pubs later. You know the sort of non-resident-Dad things."

"He must miss her, even so."

"I think she was humouring him by the end. Actually she was humouring both of us. I was looking through some photographs the other day and you can sort of see it. There's a far-away look in her eyes, as if she was already somewhere else. I couldn't pinpoint the day it happened, but I know it was some time ago. All the time she was having Sunday lunch at home with me, or going shopping, or looking at holiday brochures or paint charts for the house, in reality, she'd gone."

How many years we had with Seven before she left (17) (including the ones when she wished she was somewhere else).

"So when Rod showed up last Saturday, as if nothing had happened, I took him to the zoo."

"The zoo?"

"Well we had a day to fill and I hadn't been for years and years. It seemed like a good idea at the time."

"And was it?"

"Actually it was rather. We looked at bears and penguins and lions - I know that wasn't the right order - and monkeys because Rod wanted to, and we ate some disgusting food in the Safari Cafe, and tried to pretend that we weren't two sad divorced people who had had a child and lost her."

"You haven't lost her!"

"I know. We haven't lost Seven herself. But we've lost the child in her. Somehow, while we weren't looking, she just got away from us. And I don't think Rod has any idea how to relate to her as anything but a little girl. Poor old Rod."

The number of times we'd said 'Poor old Rod' (3000) (spread in stages of increasing frequency over twenty years).

"Was it romantic? The zoo?"

"God no. This is Rod remember? But it was surprisingly OK."

The number of times I had been surprised, in a good way (Maybe 1. Or 2) (Both recently).

The waiter brought huge plates and set them down in front of us. In the middle of each was a tiny but undeniably beautiful fig and walnut salad.

"Wow." said Jenna. "This looks good."

There was a bit of a commotion at the table next to ours and we looked up to see another waiter posed just behind a seated girl. The girl was little more than a child, she was definitely not more than seventeen. She looked like a doll, the sort all toddlers want, slightly chubby, with long fair hair in two braids and a powder-blue cardigan which matched her eyes. She had a little flowered cotton dress on, and shoes that Americans - Colin - would probably call Mary-Janes. The waiter had a bottle of champagne in his hand, he looked as though he was about to hit her over the head with it. Bit obvious I thought, Inspector Morse would have that dealt with in half an hour.

Then I noticed the young man, kneeling on the floor beside her the top of his head barely visible over the table.

An expectant hush had fallen over the restaurant. The young man whispered something, and we all strained to hear. Oh, how we longed for an eloquent proposal, words of love and honour and cherishing. The proposal of our dreams, rather than the proposals of our lives.

"What's he saying?" asked Jenna in an urgent whisper.

"I love the way you look like a beautiful doll my sister used to have," I began, "I love the way your golden hair looks in the sun. I love that you hate coffee but love coffee-flavoured things. I love the way you hold my hand in the dark and the way you look like a princess even in the morning. I love that you are brilliant and much cleverer than me and that you will always earn more than I do and I love the way you fall asleep less than halfway through any film. I promise to buy you flowers that are different every time and aren't from the garage or the supermarket and aren't spray carnations or those papery purple things that they put in to pad out the bunch. I promise to cook dinner at least once a week and fix things round the house that worry you before they get so bad you have to call a man in. I promise to be thrilled when you buy shoes and have your hair done and never be surprised at the cost. I promise never to screw our son's girlfriend on your kitchen table or share your Jo Malone bath oil with her.."

"Really?" said Jenna.

"Nope." I said.

"Do you know when Rod proposed to me, he told me about a couple he knew who paid the divers at an aquarium to put on a proposal show inside their biggest fish tank. They had a waterproof sign which read 'Will You Marry Me' and held it up against the glass."

"Wow. I'd just think of sharks." I said.

"Romantic though," she said, wistfully.

"How did Rod propose? Apart from telling you the fish story."

"I can't remember."

"It can't have been that impressive. You said No."

"It wasn't the proposal I said no to. It was marriage. Marriage is for other people. it was never for me."

"Is it for anyone, really?"

"Of course it is. It's for them. Look."

We looked. The boy was still on his knees, now proffering a small open box. The rest of the diners were surreptitiously drawing their chairs closer, craning to see the ring. Sadly nobody had a magnifying glass powerful enough.

The girl put a hand to her mouth. Then she made a sort of sighing noise. We held our collective breath, you could have heard a fork drop. This wasn't going quite the way the majority of us had hoped. There was a long, long silence.

"Tell him yes. Even if you are dying of fear, even if you are sorry later, because whatever you do, you will be sorry all the rest of your life if you say no. (Gabriel García Márquez, *Love in the Time of Cholera*)" I said, very quietly.

"Yes." she said, in a whisper.

The restaurant erupted in applause. The boy got rather awkwardly off his knees and hugged her. I must have been the only person who noticed that her eyes were closed when she hugged him back, and her tiny hands were clenched, like fists.

The number of years I give that marriage (2).

I accidentally ate my salad.

Chapter Twenty-One : Things I Have Always Known

So I had all the numbers but I hadn't quite worked out what to do with them. Should I multiply or add, or would I need a calculator?

Jenna had gone back to talking about the zoo by the time the waiters finished fannying about with Champagne and sparkler-infused cake at the next table and brought us each a tiny square of fish on a teaspoon of lentils. The size of the plates was continuing to be inversely proportional to the size of the food.

"Wow." said Jenna again, "I'm going to be full if I eat all this."

Calories in the entire meal so far (100) (and that's the combination of both our meals).

I was beginning to realise that if you used reasonable estimates for life in general, the amount of times one had been happy, the amount of fun one could have, the level of satisfaction with one's experiences, and so on, comparison with my own reality would almost certainly result in a minus number.

"So I've decided to go," said Jenna with a triumphant flourish. "Will you miss me?"

And that was when I realised that Jenna's important news was that she was leaving me. She had decided, somewhere between the gibbons and giraffes, that she had been in one place too long and she was off on a Road Trip. She said she was tired of waiting for life to come to her and she was going to go and find it. That her life was fifty percent as good as it should be and she was looking for 100 percent. That she believed she would find it on a motorbike, in Russia. Although she was planning to start in Northumberland.

"Come On," she said, which was when I realised I was crying. I had already doubled the amount of jus surrounding the halibut on my plate and I'd only been doing it for a moment.

"You know what I'm talking about, don't you?" she said, "The moment when life just tells you to get going? It's happened to you too, don't pretend it hasn't. What do you think this Colin thing is all about? It's an adventure. And what you need Jo, is a real adventure. You know you do."

Things I have always known:

1. That Greg's mother hates me. We've all pretended it isn't true, but from the moment we met. I was an ex-art student (for which she read 'drug addict') and a fledgling career woman (overpaid show-off) and a voracious reader of fiction (lazy selfish girl who would be rotten at housekeeping). Joan was a woman who seriously believed being a wife and mother was a full-time career, that people from broken homes could never be completely normal, and that bathroom fittings should be surrounded by pastel-coloured deep-pile rugs. Mutual admiration was always going to be a long shot. The vile chicken jug was just another in a series of annual symbols, graciously bestowed to make absolutely sure nobody could ever think she liked me.

2. That the people who live next door will never sell up, buy a tent and go in search of Macchu Picchu. They've been planning it for almost two decades, and every evening, at about half past six they turn on the lights in their front room, pour

themselves gin and tonics and sit down with magazines called Wondrous Walking and The World on Foot. At weekends they browse outdoor clothing shops and compare the merits of breathable clothing. Brian's nearly seventy now and he's not so good on his feet, but Dorothy still potters about the house in her thick walking socks and zip-up fleeces, talking about their Big Adventure.

3. That Hugo is gay. Oh, you've all been thinking it. How else would it be possible for another man, twice his age, to steal a sexy girl from under his nose? Why didn't he mind? Hugo hasn't told me yet, but they say a mother always knows. I pretend I don't, I even dream about his wife and children, but then something always crops up to remind me. Like just then, when Jenna was so unsurprised that the coffee shop boys reminded me of Hugo.

I don't mind at all, in fact I'm proud of him, for knowing something so definite about himself. I hope he has the confidence to see it through. Just because Icarus's wings didn't last doesn't mean he was wrong to head for the sun. As long as he's happy.

I wonder if Seven knows. Probably. The wisdom of the young never ceases to amaze me. Where does that wisdom go? Does it all get put away in a box in the attic on your wedding day?

4. That green just doesn't work for me. Olive is marginally better than emerald, jade by far the worst. My own mother looked great in green. It was another source of disappointment to her that I didn't. She kept giving me green things, a pashmina here, a cashmere cardigan there, always lovely in the bag, always terrible on. People would come up to me and ask if I felt alright. Say things like 'poor you, you've obviously got that bug that's going round'.

"I love you today Mummy," Hugo had said once, "You remind me of lettuce."

Things I never knew:

That I needed a real adventure

That one day, half way through my life, I would just get up and walk out of it. Leave it all behind.

Chapter Twenty-Two : Starting Our Descent

What are we all hoping for?

A safe landing, that's a given. Apparently landing is the second most dangerous bit of flying. Taking off is more dangerous because of all the fuel. We're all trying not to imagine what will happen when 400 tons of us hits the tarmac at 150 miles an hour. We find it hard to imagine that those little wheels will hold us up, that we won't collapse, tip, even roll over, skewing wildly, breaking up and eventually bursting into a ball of flame. We look to the crew for reassurance, as they trundle their trolleys up and down again, collecting the vast amount of rubbish we seem to have accumulated, and pouring out terrible tin-tasting tea and coffee.

Why does everything on an aeroplane come wrapped in plastic? The pillow, the blanket, the headphones, all the food, magazines, it all generates mountains of completely non-recyclable waste which spreads around us, spills into the aisles and under the seats, fills pockets and crevices, and must eventually be removed and presumably deposited in our destination country, a sort of 'arrival gift' along with hundreds of tired grey and slightly malodorous people who haven't filled out the appropriate paperwork, or who at least have not filled it out properly, and whose tempers and minds are frayed by lack of clean air and sleep.

Welcome to America, thank you so much for bringing us all that rubbish.

Malcolm is properly awake again. He is dusting everything off, like an overenthusiastic housekeeper who has been trapped in a cupboard. He brushes against me rather more often than I would think is necessary. What is he hoping for, I wonder. A rapidly moving taxi queue so he can get back to his apartment on the corner of Morton and Washington as soon as possible? Probably a shower, some clean clothes, and, a pat and a walk for Barney before heading out into the Village, a fairly attractive, (oh alright, really quite attractive) single man who presumably has an address book filled with the numbers of women keen to go to dinner with him. Maybe I should be one of those women. It would do no harm to be in the address book of a good looking gentleman friend on arrival into my destination New Life. As back up, in case – well, just in case. I consider asking Malcolm if he is busy this evening, in his Village. I can always cancel, if everything's alright, if there is someone there to meet me. But is that fair? What if Malcolm took me seriously, what if he minded if I cancelled? He seems so much nicer than he did eight hours ago. Perhaps it's the altitude.

The happy couple in the seats in front of me are presumably hoping to find a bed. I hope so. Without one, they run the risk of being arrested for affront to public decency once we land.

The married-with-a-lover-each couple will be hoping for distractions, so they don't have to face one another. They probably have friends in the City, people who they've known their whole married life, people who just by behaving as usual will reassure them that their marriage is still alive. They will follow an itinerary, go to the right places, eat out, walk, meet other people, maybe go to some parties.

And they will manage skilfully, and after a great deal of practice to go through days without having a whole, exclusive conversation with one another. And if they don't have a conversation they can't get into a row, and if they don't get into a row they can't accidentally and explosively and irretrievably confess to having lovers, people who Do appreciate them, people who Do understand them, people who Don't take them for granted or Treat them like hotel staff.

The baby couple are just hoping that this last final effort will result in their wish being granted. They have already risked the disapproval of their friends and family, and have heard the tales of woe and disaster that have apparently befallen others who have taken this route to parenthood. They know all the facts and the statistics, and they know the risks and they are pretty nearly bankrupt over it all, but they are still hopeful. Jade, a twenty-seven year old mother of five from Wisconsin, has already been a surrogate to two other families, and has come to them through a reputable agency. What can go wrong?

'Americans', say their friends and in particular, the girl's mother. They're not like us. They do things differently there.

There is a tiny old lady about two rows back on the aisle. I hadn't noticed her before, everything else on this plane has hidden her from view. She's dressed in purple, from head to foot, and if I'm not mistaken, she is wearing a small feathered hat. After eight hours on this long haul flight, she still has her hat on. All credit to the woman I say. She must be a hundred years old, and her skin looks paper-thin. She looks like an antique doll, the kind you see in the window of dusty old bric-a-brac shops in forgotten market towns. Why is she going to New York, I wonder, what is left for her to hope for?

Perhaps the Statue of Liberty is the only great monument in the world she hasn't seen. Or maybe she is visiting her huge, fat, wealthy banker of a grandson to see if she wants to leave him her small house in Hove. Or maybe she will buy jewellery on Fifth Avenue, and take a carriage ride in Central Park before drinking champagne at the Carlyle for the last time, in memory of a long lost love. Perhaps she is me, half a century on.

Shane and Wendy are just hoping for a quick transit through the airport, no problem passengers, no lost baggage, no mix up with the stop-over arrangements. Wendy has been drafted into a double date by Pam in First Class, who has fixed herself up with one of a two-man delegation to a conference on sub-prime lending risk on Wall Street. This is a great result for Wendy, after her disappointment with Malcolm, and a subsequent knock-back from a bookshop chain director who is flying home to an apartment on the Upper West Side, and who looked most promising until he told her about his Civil Partner. Funny, Shane said when Wendy told him, he doesn't look gay. Shane is as disappointed as Wendy, for that surely was a missed opportunity.

(Later Shane will hook up with a Pan-Am crew who are partying in the Meatpacking District. He will only narrowly make his return flight tomorrow evening).

And me, the middle-aged woman in a creased skirt and shirt, whose lined face looks sadly back at me in the harsh light of the cabin after the longest eight hours of my life, what am I hoping for?

The week after Colin left me at Le Manoir and headed back to Broadway, I worked incredibly hard to take my mind off him. I stopped drifting about and cleaned the house from top to bottom, throwing out bag after bag of junk, the stuff of an eighteen-year marriage, things belonging to the grown man who used to be my child, and the sort of things houses just seem to accumulate without their owners being aware of it: tea services, (never used – who uses a tea service?) odd mugs of indeterminate origin, unused gadgetry, drawers and drawers full of old batteries and keys and string cut into useless lengths. Long discarded Christmas decorations, and empty tins and boxes which were once too pretty to throw away but are now battered and faded, and ornaments which were never anything but dreadful. I threw away boxes of soap which were so old they smelled of old cupboards, and I took tablecloths to charity shops. When did I ever think I would use a tablecloth, still less one with a mysterious stain in the middle of it? I threw away jigsaws with missing pieces, and missing pieces without jigsaws, Hugo's toys, and single shoes, and misshapen lampshades, and then I threw out things which were fine, but I just didn't like them, more plates, nasty ties which Greg insisted on wearing, lots of brown things, any towels and sheets which weren't white or cream, more drawers full of leaky pens and handfuls of loose paperclips and elastic bands, and then I threw out Hugo's favourite tracksuit which he had left under his bed for a year and he was devastated and I had to go back to the charity shop and get it back.

And after all that, I looked round my shabby house and thought, well at least it's mine, and it's pretty and in a great place, and Hugo and Greg are here and don't have any terrible illnesses, and Christmas is coming. So I counted my blessings, and tried so very hard not to think about Colin Pitt and the fact that he hadn't called or written to me. The count of my blessings was eight:

My house is nice

My son loves me
Neither my husband nor my son is ill
I am not ill
Christmas is coming
My best friend is always there for me
I am not as fat as I used to be
I know who the love of my life is.

And then I came home from my lunch with Jenna and the count was reduced to seven because she was leaving me, and then six because the house wasn't anything like as nice as before, especially the bathroom because it still reminded me of Lucie. And after that I realized that I did have a bad illness, and it was called loneliness and despair. I ate doughnuts and drank wine, so I was bound to have put on half a stone, so the count was down to four.

I wrote to Colin. I wrote him a long letter, all about how much I missed him, and how magical our time had been and how I treasured my little champagne glass which was next to my heart, although he was right in my heart, and all about Oxfordshire in the sunshine and how he had brought the sunshine back to my life and so on, and so on, and then I threw it away, and wrote him a hilariously funny email about overhearing some people on a bus where one had asked the other if she had ever been to Peru and the other one thought she said Crewe and the multitude of misunderstandings that followed, and then I deleted the email by mistake and when I tried to write it again it didn't seem so hilarious.

All this time Greg was pretending that nothing had happened, and it seemed easier if I did too. He said he wasn't seeing Lucie any more, and I put all the Jo Malone away in my secret cupboard and bought some really nasty cheap bubble bath from a supermarket which would leave your body feeling like you'd been sitting in washing-up water for a week. Just in case.

Greg and I continued to go to the supermarket once or twice a week, and bought the things we always had. He went to work and came back and ate whatever I'd cooked. We watched cookery shows and property shows on the TV in the kitchen, and if Hugo was in, Greg and he watched football and boxing on the TV in the sitting room. Greg remembered my birthday, which was quite unusual, given that I hadn't bothered with the post-it note and fridge magnet reminders, and he bought me a stick blender.

And I went to sleep each night looking out of the window at the stars and concentrating on what time it was in New York, and what Colin might be doing, and holding my champagne glass charm in my hand.

Rod called me one morning, as I was hoovering again. We had one of those bagless upright hoovers which are so effective that I hardly knew if the carpet was clean or not because so much of it was in the hoover. He said Jenna was in Newcastle, on a Harley Davidson, and that she'd asked me to call her. Apparently she'd had a vision about me, flying through the air on a stick blender. Well, that was spooky.

"I thought I might take a holiday," I said to Rod. "To New York. I've never been."

"I'll let her know," he said, "she worries about you you know? We both do."

Jenna sent me an email that night.

"Freedom's just another word for nothing left to lose," it said.

"Thanks," I emailed back.

"Don't thank me, thank Kris Kristofferson."

"Maybe I just want too much?"

"Your problem is you don't want enough. You've spent your whole life believing that some is enough, that alright is alright, that near enough is near enough. Desperado."

"Desperado?"

"Come to your senses, come down from your fences, and let somebody love you, before it's too late."

God, Newcastle's changed. I thought.

Well, what was I supposed to do? I only had four blessings left and she was one of them. I could hardly ignore what she said, could I?

So in the end, I booked my flight online, and sent an email to Colin, which just said ' Virgin Atlantic 566' and the date and the proposed landing time. And I used clip-art to put a little picture of a champagne glass on it.

I gave Greg to Lucie as a present. I found a photograph of him on a beach, in those huge orange beach shorts, the ones Hugo said made him look like a tosser. Then I put it in an old frame, and tied a pink bow round it and sent it round to Lucie, at her mother's house, with a message saying Happy Fortieth Birthday, just so she'd know what it felt like to be the right age for Greg.

I just wanted to be helpful.

Chapter Twenty-Three : Down

Even though we all know it will take a long time to land, we carry on tidying ourselves up. We each make our tiny area habitable again, like hamsters preparing for hibernation, or an elderly schoolmistress getting ready to greet an important visitor, folding and tucking, and brushing, until we each sit upright, in our own neat little spaces, for all the world as though we hadn't spent the last eight hours snoring, dribbling, having sex, eating out of plastic tubs, and watching B-grade sitcoms and unsuitably violent films.

Below us, I can feel the hugeness of America. A new continent, a new world, and in every sense for me, a new life. I have truly cast off the bounds of Oxfordshire, England, Europe, and I have made it Out.

We hear the wheels go down from underneath us, note that they lock with a reassuring grind and clunk, and we smile at one another, as if to say, oh, this is nothing, I do this all the time. Looking down from my window, I can see the airport in the distance, a vast spider with a square sprawling body, and legs which spread out straight in all directions, claiming the land beneath.

As we approach, the ground appears to rise up to meet us, and after a heavy bounce, there is a piercing screech and a huge cloud of burning rubber enfolds us, as we shudder wildly across the runway and eventually, only just in time it seems, come to a halt. Is that how it was supposed to go? I wonder.

I've heard there are flights where the passengers are so thrilled to have landed safely that they applaud. Here, there is just a collective sigh of relief, and then a sudden scrambling as people leap out of their seats, despite having been expressly told not to do so by Captain Carlton. Those of us who fly frequently (Malcolm) and those of us who tend on the whole to do as they are told (me) remain in our seats, as the huge plane lumbers clumsily round a corner and drives towards a vacant parking place in the line of aircraft already humming away, like dinosaurs being fed through the embarkation tubes which attach them to the terminal building.

Malcolm and I look politely at one another, as if to say, 'These people, how ridiculous they are. Everyone can see there is no point in getting up until the aircraft engines have been switched off and seat belt signs extinguished'. Mobile phones ring all round us, and the air is alive with 'I've just landed' conversations.

By the time the door is opened, there are so many people are standing in the aisles that I can't see beyond our Row. I can however feel the huge wave of fresh air which makes its way rapidly through the plane. It is cold, and clean, and I have a vision of an equal sized cloud of hot purple, poisonous air escaping into the atmosphere from us, in its place. I imagine the purple cloud hovering for a moment above us, waiting for every last feeble atom to be squeezed out by the good fresh strong air of suburban New York, before taking itself off in the direction of the wind, away towards Newfoundland, where a flock of hardy sheep will eventually look up and do whatever sheep do instead of frowning , and think to themselves, 'the air's a bit off today, you know what this smells like? It smells like 400 Europeans who have been trapped in a tin can for eight hours.'

The crowd in the aisles begins to thin out, and Malcolm tries to stand up. Suddenly I am afraid.

The crew is keen to get us all off. They are marshalling people towards the doors, grabbing things from overhead lockers and thrusting them at their owners, almost shovelling us along the plane. They know that as soon as we are all safely inside the airport, they too can leave, and get out into some really good layover activity in the City that Never Sleeps. Right now I feel as though I have never slept.

Shane is smiling like a Cheshire cat, saying goodbye to every single man, woman and child as though he is a favourite uncle, brother, son. "See you again soon!" he trills, barely refraining from making very different faces behind the backs of the more demanding customers. Wendy, although trying her best to do the same, is channeling the look of a serial killer. Behind her, Captain Carlton and the flight deck team can be seen through the now-open door to the driving seat, packing their plastic lunchboxes and paperbacks into their briefcases and retrieving their much-braided hats from under the seats. There seems to be some sort of sign language going on, I imagine this has more to do with layover promises than comments about the flight. I hear someone referring to "Tommy two-Wheels" and receiving a side swipe from an aviation manual in return. More flight crew are sweeping the passengers from the back of the plane in a rear guard action.

Suddenly I don't want to leave. This plane, with its tiny seats and its awful nylon upholstery, its overheated air and its underheated tea, Malcolm, with his pin striped bulk and dangerous suggestions, the little plastic packets of food, it all seems like home, and everything else, everything 'out there' appears threatening, full of dangers waiting to strike. Malcolm has already left me behind, I catch sight of his retreating back a good few people ahead of me, and I feel naked, far more exposed without him than I contemplated being with him. I can see Shane advancing towards me, his 'I'll smile and smile until you get off this bloody plane' look fixed firmly across his perma-tanned face.

My jacket, as he hands it to me from the overhead locker, is, as I predicted, crushed beyond recognition.

"Oh dear" he says, "that's seen better days hasn't it? I know someone who'll be hitting Fifth Avenue this afternoon!"

As I progress along the aisle, I see I am not quite the last to leave the plane. Behind me, a harassed woman with two sleepy children is dragging them by reluctant arms up behind me, trailing bags and sweaters. She looks exhausted, as though this journey, the few yards of airline carpet towards the wide open space that is America, may well be her last. I wonder what she is going towards. Is she, like me, is somewhere between escaping and running for her life? I smile reassuringly at her but she doesn't notice. Presumably she has no energy left for anything that isn't actually essential for survival. One of her two children sticks its tongue out at me.

So we all make our weary, grubby way into the terminal, and eventually, some five hundred miles of glass-sided rubber-floored walkway later, we are all reunited, in the queue for Immigration. All around us, high above the vast hall, there are posters advertising the wonderful things one can look forward to in The Big Apple. Diners, restaurants, broadway shows, off-broadway shows, new movies opening all over town, cocktail bars and nightclubs, department stores, bookstores, beware of pickpockets, don't pick up an unlicensed cab, don't carry a gun or the police will shoot you, Remember 9/11, and McDonalds.

On the other side of this queue, is America. The land of movie stars and cop dramas, and big food. I am very small.

The queue moves incredibly slowly. It seems we must each have an in-depth interview with Wanda diMarco (the inhabitant of the glass booth at the head of the queue I'm in) or one of her equally sizeable and all-powerful colleagues, before we can be allowed into America. What is it they hope to discover at this point? I wonder. We have all come so far, (some much further than others), to be here. What would happen if they sent any of us away? We don't want you in America, you must go back to where you came from. What of those who cannot go back, who have irrevocably, totally permanently, left? 'Sorry Greg, I went to America, for ever, but they wouldn't let me in. Hope that's OK, and what do you want for supper?'

Why would America want me? Nobody else does. Except Colin, for a bit. I think he wanted me. I hope he did, indeed I hope he still does, now I've come all this way. Perhaps that's good enough. Perhaps I will say to Wanda diMarco, 'You may not think much of me, a tired middle-aged woman in a dreadfully creased linen jacket, but one of your citizens has specially requested me.'

I spot Malcolm in the adjacent queue. He looks smaller too, standing in this big queue to get into this big country. His queue is for US Citizens, but it doesn't seem to be moving any more quickly. I wonder what they ask them. 'Where have you been? why did you go? did you think anywhere would be better than America? Have you brought us back a present?'

I smile encouragingly at Malcolm. After all, he did propose a very intimate encounter, and he is the only person I know in America. To my astonishment, he completely ignores me. Surely, it can't be that he doesn't recognize me? I probably look a bit smaller, now that I am standing in a much bigger space, and my jacket isn't at its best, but otherwise I'm the same, the very woman he nearly had sex with in an aircraft lavatory, the woman he talked to about his dog, his apartment, his bachelor life. I decide he's short sighted, and wave.

Malcolm pretends to be reading his passport.

Which is ridiculous. Everyone knows what their passport says. That stuff about the Geneva convention, and who to contact in case of an emergency. A few stamps, your date of birth, nothing that the passport holder doesn't know already. The only joy in reading passports is in reading other people's and commenting on the photographs. You know the joke, if you look like your passport photograph you're too ill to travel. I look like my old school caretaker in mine. Derek Chisolm, his name was.

I begin to be aware that I'm not the only one isolated from the crowd here. Despite the fact that only a couple of hours ago, we were all sleeping together, we are now complete strangers again. Nobody is associating with anyone else, unless they were together in the first place, and even they, the couples and groups, are seemingly being pretty cagey about what they do or say. There is a lot of nodding, and nudging and pointing going on.

I suppose it makes sense. After all, you never know with complete strangers, who you're associating with do you? I can see sweaty guy up ahead. He's trying too hard to fit in, so I notice him immediately, and am cruelly glad that he isn't in my queue. I start to add up the possible issues that will arise as each of the people ahead of me meets Wanda. They are mostly single men, business types, that's why I chose this queue, they're all seasoned travellers, they'll whip through. There is a rather dishevelled teenage boy I'm a bit worried about, he's the type to have lost his green visa waiver form, or to make a stupid joke about bombers. And there's the very old lady too, she's moving very, very slowly. I hope she can see over the counter, and that she lasts until she gets to the other side, an incident involving a medical team would really hold us up.

And yet, all this is really more about my own sense of the need for efficiency than it is an anxiety to get through myself. I'm not sure I'm in any sort of hurry now. I'm not at all sure I want to run away to America at all.

Another half hour has passed. Now it's just me, the big yellow line and Wanda diMarco. She towers above me like a juggernaut in the fast lane, there's nothing between us except a couple of feet of bulletproof glass. A number of cameras are trained on me. I feel as though I should confess something but my mind has gone completely blank. In fact it's gone so blank I can't remember the name of the small boutique hotel I booked on the internet a couple of days ago, just in case. In case of what? When I booked it, I told myself it was in case I needed to freshen up on the way to the Bubble Lounge.

I can't remember my own name either. Wanda is unimpressed. She asks me how long I plan to stay in 'Nork', and that's a question I couldn't answer even if I hadn't lost my memory entirely.

"It all depends you see," I begin. She looks at me very sternly indeed.

"You have a return ticket." she points out. "You have a visitor's visa waiver which gives you exactly three months, not a day more. If you ain't tired of the sights by then, too bad lady, you're on your way home. You wanna stay? You have to apply for an immigrant visa. Will you get lucky? Who knows?"

She stamps my passport several times with such force that my feet leave the ground. Then she shoves it across the desk at me. I look at her blankly.

"Whatever you lookin' for lady, you aint gonna find it standin' there lookin' at me like a cow in a sandstorm," she says, and then she shouts, "Next in Line!" and I am in America, ready or not.

Chapter Twenty-Four : In Which Words Fail Me

What do you say to a man you've been married to for twenty years? When you're on your way out of the house you've shared for most of those years, and you're never coming back?

I'd left it a bit late to write the letter really. As I rummaged about in a kitchen drawer for a bit of clean paper and a pen that actually worked, my jacket already on, and the time until my taxi arrived ticking away the few remaining minutes, I realised I had no idea what I was going to write. It would be too much to hope for that any kind of poetic muse might strike me at the last minute.

I didn't want to bring up the whole Lucie thing. In the end it wasn't really about her, and besides I should have hated for her to take the credit for anything I did. She'll have to make her own life, have her own adventures. I don't imagine Greg will feature in them, but you never know. One of Greg's fifty-something golfing friends now spends several hours a week in fertility clinics in an effort to hang onto his thirty-something girlfriend, by giving her a baby, while the children from his first marriage refuse to acknowledge her existence, mainly because she was in the year below them at secondary school.

I wanted to write something meaningful but I couldn't really think of anything. Meaningful wasn't really what our marriage was about, we didn't really do meaningful. Our years together had been about domestic arrangements, and felt pen messages on kitchen calendars, about successive Christmases, always the same, and the annual summer holiday, two weeks in a holiday cottage in Pembrokeshire, walking vaguely about on windswept beaches and trying to find pubs which had made it into the twenty-first century to eat in. I'd suggested Italy one year but somehow we never got around to it. Our years were about successive seasons of reality television shows, and remembering to put the recycling out.

When I tried to think of the significant things about our marriage, I failed to come up with any. The years had just gone by, round and round, on and on, like slow moving traffic in the rain on the ring road.

The supermarket receipt I'd found to write on wasn't big enough for significant statements either, exhortations to seize the day, or calls for him to slip the surly bonds of Earth. So in the end I just wrote.:

I've gone to America. I don't think I'll want to come back. I hope you'll be OK. Jo x

Chapter Twenty-Five : Reclamation

As we all gather round the luggage conveyor, pretending we are completely cool about whether our luggage will appear, and not in any sort of hurry, we try to look relaxed. Sheepish grins are allowed, the odd smile. Immigration was a dreadful ordeal but we are all through it. We are in America, and we are either home, or the beginning of an adventure. One of the weary mother's children is lying on the carousel. As he passes regally by, legs and arms in the air, she is probably hoping that someone else will haul him off before he goes back through the rubber strips and out via the chute onto the runway. Luckily it is a long way round, so his chances are reasonably good.

We crane our necks and edge and shuffle, fingers crossed in the alien atmosphere, that our own luggage, the only possessions we have in the world, will appear through the hatch, still in one piece, and we will be reunited. Visions of lone items of unsavoury underwear scattered from a broken suitcase, passing along the route on display to all fill our heads. I'm looking for my extremely ordinary black canvas case, with its scuff marks caused by Hugo's tatty ski-ing boots which were attached by the handle on a student rail trip, and the splash of white gloss paint which missed the doorframe when the suitcase cupboard was refurbished. Just before I left the house I attached a length of rainbow ribbon through the little holes in both zip pulls, I wonder if that too will have made the journey.

Smugly, one passenger after another drags a bag off the carousel, and onto a trolley, and heads, possessions reclaimed and piled high, towards the customs clearance channel and out and away. We are all acutely aware of being watched by the banks of CCTV cameras above us, but with each stage we get through we feel lighter, more relieved. Like contestants in a giant televised obstacle race, we tackle each massive multi-coloured hurdle as it comes, and scaling its heights, slide down the other side, joyful, triumphant, ready for the next one.

At last I notice my rainbow ribbon, bedraggled, knotted, rather sorry for itself but still clinging valiantly to my case, which is itself sandwiched between two vast matching designer trunks, which will later be claimed by a representative of somebody who was sitting in First Class. I manage to haul it out, just before it is dragged out of my hands by the motion of the conveyor, and although I am surrounded by decent-sized men, all gazing determinedly into the middle distance, I manage to do it by myself. Lugging it onto the floor, and then onto a trolley with decidedly wayward wheels, I straighten myself out and head for Customs. With each step I am closer to the other side. For the first time I am faced with the very real question of whether or not Colin will be there.

I stride in what I believe is a confident (but not over-confident) way, along a white-painted tunnel with its two way mirrors on all sides. I can see myself all round, lit by the ugly overhead neon, I look grey, shabby, guilty. They can see me, but I can't see them. They can see through me, they know the very thoughts of my heart, they can probably see my heart beating harder and faster as I go. I just hope they are sufficiently well trained to know the difference between a drug smuggler and a woman who has run away from home and is on her way to meet a lover.

I read an article once, written by a customs officer, in which he said that in addition to a constant list of suspects they are primed to look out for and apprehend, they are also encouraged to stop passengers at random, just to get the message across, to scare the living daylights out of people like me who feel guilty even when they haven't done anything wrong . And in order to do this random stopping, they tend to work with hunches, and those hunches are fed by anomalies, those little things which attach to a few of us, little things which set us apart from others. A hat for example, I remember he was particularly insistent about hats. They always warrant a search apparently, as do people going on long holidays with no luggage, or short holidays with masses of bags. There, now I am teaching other people how to avoid being detected in the process of perpetrating a Crime.

I have normal luggage. I have no hat. In front of me is a family of four with a holdall each, and a single girl with eight cases. Neither of them is called over. It's going to be me, I just know it is. It's so unfair. I've done nothing wrong, I can't even step on a beetle without feeling so guilty I have to confess it to the first person I see. I can't even keep loose change I find in ticket machines, or – oh.

Across the room, I see Mr Sweaty being pulled over by a customs official. Bluff double bluffed. I'm so busy wondering what will happen to him that I barely realize I have got all the way through the Customs Channel unstopped. I suppose all that sweat of his represents an anomaly of sorts, It really isn't that hot in here.

The opaque glass electronic doors to the outside world slide open with a swish, and I can see down a long glass corridor, into the Arrivals Hall. I dare not look, but as I slow my stride, I am overtaken by a large-ish man in a pin striped suit, who is almost running down the slope towards a small boy in long shorts wearing a baseball hat. The child throws his arms around the man's neck and he stands, bringing the child up level with his face, hugging and kissing him. Then, still carrying the child, he advances down the slope towards an extremely pretty woman in a floral dress who is carrying another, rather smaller child. Standing in the slanting sunlight which bisects the Arrivals hall they look like the perfect All-American family sent in its entirety from Central Casting. The woman is laughing. The man is Malcolm.

The rest of the world spins for a minute, and I am forced to stop and sit on my case, which sags slightly in sympathy with my heart.

It's not as though I wanted Malcolm. After all, you can hardly feel someone belongs to you on the strength of an eight hour flight and nearly having sex in a very small lavatory. But somehow I do feel a bit cheated. No, it's more than that. I feel bereft. The Malcolm I knew doesn't exist. He lied to me. The first person I actually met after I set out from home, heading for my big new life, and he's a complete bloody fake.

I wish I'd lied too. I wish I'd pretended to be someone interesting, a writer perhaps or a composer, or a very important scientist. I wish I'd pretended to be rich, a philanthropist who gave away all her money so she had to travel in Economy. Or a painter, on her way to an exhibition in a Gallery on the Upper East Side. (Rough Guide says that's where all the best private galleries are.) At any rate I do not wish I'd gone through with the mile-high thing. Imagine. As I look down to where that pretty woman is still standing, her family all around her, her hair shining in the sun, how would I have felt?

I may not be a writer or a composer or a scientist or a painter, but at least I'm not a husband-stealing tart.

The happy family collects itself together and heads towards the exit doors on the far side of the terminal, the child skipping behind his father, Malcolm's arm protectively round the floral woman's waist, the baby cradled between them. And I just sit there.

"Excuse me!" says an imperious voice. "But you are rather obstructing this walkway"

I look round to see where this big voice is coming from and find myself staring right into the eyes of the tiny old lady in the purple hat. Although the next thing I notice is that it is not a purple feathered hat at all, it is purple hair. And the next thing I notice is what can only be described as a rucksack, almost as large as its wearer, hoisted manfully onto her back.

"Are you unwell?" the voice enquires.

"No, no, not really. I'm just, I'm just...." my own voice trails away.

"Scared? Let down, disappointed? Not what you had in mind? Well, Welcome to the club dear. We're all scared, and we're all disappointed. But what I always say, is meet trouble head on, and it'll probably run away. I find it usually does."

I can believe it. I think your average bout of ferocious-toothed evil-intentioned trouble would baulk at meeting this formidable old thing head-on. I pick up my case, trying to pretend it is weightless for me, a woman a third my companion's age, and instantly feel as though I have put my back out.

"Jolly good," she says firmly, and strides past me, down the slope, across the terminal. I watch her in the distance, a tiny little mauve bird with its heavy load held aloft, hailing a taxi from the middle of the road. I can hear the distant sounds of hooting and screeching of tyres, shouts of "Hey lady! You wanna die here?"

How can I have been so wrong? Wrong about Malcolm, wrong about bird lady.

What if I am wrong about everything? Wrong about Greg and Lucie, wrong about leaving? What if I'm not having a mid-life crisis at all, but am just behaving very badly? And oh what of whats, what if I am wrong about Colin?

I start to walk again, one foot in front of the other, meeting trouble head on. I can't see Colin, as I scan the heads in the still-expectant crowd, with its notices and welcome banners and excitable relatives. But just because I can't see him, doesn't mean he isn't there. Does it?

THE END

MID-ATLANTIC

DID YOU ENJOY MID-ATLANTIC?

Tora would be very grateful if you would leave an honest review on Amazon UK or Amazon US. Reviews make all the difference to independent authors, and help us to write more of the books you love, as well as reaching new readers.

You can read more about Tora Barry by visiting her website www.torabarry.com. If you choose to subscribe to her news update service, you'll be the first to hear about new books, promotions and give-aways.

You can also follow Tora on twitter: @torabarrywriter

ACKNOWLEDGMENTS

Special thanks to Lucy Barry, sister and clever cover designer, to my first readers and relentless champions, Alexis Thompson and Caryl Hodgson, to Izzy Hodgson for her particular input as to the ending, and to JKEH, for working ridiculous hours in far-away places to allow me to sit at home in my pyjamas, writing.

TORA BARRY